3

3

Dead Man Running

Dead Man Running

ROY LEWIS

This edition published in Great Britain in 2003 by
Allison & Busby Limited
Bon Marche Centre
241-251 Ferndale Road
Brixton, London SW9 8BJ
http://www.allisonandbusby.com

A catalogue record for this book is available from the British Library

ISBN 0 7490 0677 3

Printed and bound by
Creative Print + Design, Ebbw Vale, Wales

ROY LEWIS is a Welshman who now lives in the north of England where he sets many of his books. He is also the author of the Arnold Landon series of mysteries.

Prologue

The clouds had massed heavily in the eastern sky and the moonlight that had earlier bathed the hills in a pale, ethereal shimmer had become shadowed, deep-recessed across the rolling farmland that lay about them. As they waited silently a menacing flicker of lightning briefly edged the clouds with silver and after a few seconds there was a vague rumble of thunder in the air. On the distant hill, lights twinkled from a farm across the fell, beyond the deep-cut river bank; a cool breeze rustled in the hedgerow and down the valley echoed the lugubrious call of an owl, a swooping, ghostly night predator seeking its prey in the darkness. The sound sent a quick, involuntary shiver down Detective Sergeant Chris Jarrad's spine, as though some old-shaped instinct reminded him that in the countryside the eerie hooting of a solitary owl could presage death.

But he was no countryman. City-born and bred, his twenty years service with the police had largely been spent in Leeds, and Liverpool and Middlesbrough, before he had moved here, further north. At Leeds there had been forays enough into the moorland that hung above the towns, chasing car thieves and illegal immigrants in hijacked lorries but in Liverpool and Middlesbrough he had mainly dealt with villains who plied their trades on the city streets. And he had seen most of the possible kinds of action, over the years: credit fraud and corporate misdemeanours in Leeds, burglary, drugs and related violence on Middlesbrough streets, gun wars and murder in Liverpool. He had seen his share of violence, and had gained a reputation for dealing with it with a cold competence. He was a man who believed in getting his retaliation in first. There had been times when it had got him into trouble with his superiors, but he treated their occasional carpetings with disdain, for he knew they would still use him again in difficult situations where violence might occur.

Not that he was expecting much of that on this night-shadowed, lonely, wind-swept hill in the wilds of Northumberland. He had been working here a matter of months only, the area was still unfamiliar to him, and he had no feeling for the landscape. Indeed, he felt a certain contempt for the slow-speaking farmers he had met since he joined the force up here, and certainly the task he had been assigned to this evening was new to him.

It was all a far cry from the narrow, malodorous alleys he had frequented behind the city streets where he had learned his trade: a dark sky piling up with storm clouds, the tang of salt in his nostrils drifting in from the distant sea, acres of empty farmland stretching around him where he stood on the muddy rutted track. Unfamiliar sounds came to him in the darkness-muted sounds of shuffling cattle in the barn across to his left, a nocturnal scurrying in the hedgerow, a swishing of sudden wings, perhaps a buzzard sweeping above his head, and still the mournful, lonely note of the distant owl echoing down the valley.

Ahead of him, lights gleamed in the complex of barns at the end of the muddy track, glinting through the interstices of the galvanised iron walls. There was a confusion of sounds from within, the murmur of voices, swearing; a stamping of men moving about, the uneasy shifting of a group of animals crammed into crowded pens, and when one of the barn doors opened briefly a bright shaft of light split the muddied yard. A man stepped out, cleared his throat, hawked, spat and looked about him at the troubled night sky. He was broad, heavy in the shoulders, slow-moving, but with the light behind him his features could not be made out. He lit a cigarette, the match flaring behind his shielding hand, drew deeply, and coughed. He wore a donkey-jacket, and heavy boots. He stood there for a little while, dragging urgently on the cigarette, leaning against the barn door. Jarrad stayed motionless in the darkness, shadowed by the hedge, waiting with the others. After a while someone called out angrily inside the barn, the man at the door turned his head and gestured in reply, flicked the cigarette out into the yard. As it whirled away in a brief, gleaming arc he wiped an arm across his forehead, turned, and stumped his way back into the barn, slamming the door shut behind him.

Chris Jarrad wrinkled his nose as the strong, nauseating smell drifted across to him from the barn, a combination of petrol and scorched flesh. He glanced at the luminous face of his watch. He swore under his breath. The rest of the raiding group were late. He had two officers with him, but he was under orders to wait for back-up from Ponteland. Not that trouble was expected. If they found what they were looking for, they'd have a case, and, caught bang to rights, it was likely that the men involved would put up little resistance to the collar.

He looked back down the track. He thought he caught the faint rumble of an engine on the night air; dimmed headlights swept briefly across the hill and then were cut. He waited impatiently and after a while picked up the gleam of a torch; he narrowed his eyes in the darkness and sure enough, in a few seconds there was another gleam. The others were arriving, making their stumbling way up the steep, rutted track, risking an occasional flash of the torch to guide them on their way, while they left the police van at the end of the country lane.

Jarrad heaved a sigh; his heart rate began to increase at the prospect of the action that was to come.

Feet squelched in mud. He heard the sound of someone slipping, cursing. Then as the vague group emerged into view he heard a hoarse whisper from the men coming up the track. "They still in there?"

Jarrad kept his own voice low. "Far as I can make out. Don't know how many. You took your bloody time."

"Hell of a place to find, this farm. But better late than never. You all set?"

"We all go in at the front end of the barn. Doesn't seem to be any rear entrance. How many of you are there?"

"Three."

Six police officers in all. Apart from the driver, who would be back at the van, waiting for the signal to come up the track. That should be enough to cope with any trouble that might unexpectedly arise. But Jarrad guessed this would be no big deal: slow-witted, slow-moving farm labourers, he thought contemptuously, they'd probably be scared out of their wits. He waved an arm. Time to move.

The bunched group stepped cautiously out of the lane, making their way along the verge of the grassy ditch, through the open farm gate and into the empty, concreted yard in front of the barn. Parked at one side of the barn were two lorries, dark, no drivers, empty. The raiding group ignored them, walking forward towards the barn door. As they grew closer the sounds from within seemed to become more confused, a shuffling and stamping and swearing and occasional terrified bleating. The smell Jarrad had earlier picked up now became more powerful, sickeningly sweet and yet pungent, and he heard one of the men behind him swear under his breath. One of the officers at the back gagged, cleared his throat.

The six men bunched in a tight group at the barn door, waiting. Someone inside the barn had raised his voice, yelling and swearing at a companion; Jarrad glanced around at his own group, nodded, put out his hand, grasped the door and dragged it open. He led the way into the stinking interior of the barn.

Jarrad had seen the inside of drug dens, the mayhem at a multiple murder scene, the grisly remains to be discovered at an arson attack upon an Asian family who had been burned to death. But, twenty years in the service and he had never seen anything like this. He heard one of the men behind him gasp; for Jarrad it was like a mediaeval vision of hell. The barn was long and narrow, erratically lit by two spot lamps running from a generator. The atmosphere was thick with acrid smoke, a heavy dark pall hanging near the ceiling. At the far end of the partly shadowed barn was a crowded pen, where terrified animals milled about, shuffling, stamping, rolling eyes wild with fear. And between the police officers and the pens were the carcasses of more than a hundred sheep. There was a pile of animals lying sprawled about, throats cut, mostly dead, some still kicking spasmodically, blood and guts gushing onto the filthy straw that littered the earth floor of the barn. Other animals were already hanging from the walls, hooks driven through their necks, legs splayed out, the carcasses all displaying a strange, vivid golden colour, glimpsed through a haze of blue-black smoke, accompanied by an overpowering smell of burning flesh, skin and wool in the makeshift slaughter-house.

Everything suddenly seemed to have stopped for Chris Jarrad. It was a frozen tableau: the piles of slaughtered sheep, the six police officers standing, gaping in the doorway; the four men turned to look at them in surprise, against a background of the crowded pens that themselves seemed to have fallen silent momentarily. Then the sounds came sifting back in to Jarrad's senses until they seemed to roar in his ears: the stamping and shuffling and bleating of the animals, the fierce gushing of the blowtorches held by two of the men. As they stared at him, shocked, silent, he held up a gloved hand.

His voice was dry, hoarse. "All right lads. Caper's over."

The big man with the donkey jacket, whom Jarrad had seen earlier at the barn door, was the first to move, backing away towards the corner of the barn. He held a skinning knife in his hand, its long, stained blade gleaming dully. Jarrad watched him warily as the other officers stepped deeper into the barn at his back, fanning out in a menacing group. After a moment the donkey-jacketed man seemed to become aware of the knife in his hand. He raised it uncertainly.

"Don't even *think* about it, man," Jarrad warned coldly.

There was a long period of silence, but then it was as Jarrad had expected. The warning was enough. The man hesitated, licked nervous lips, then reluctantly tossed the knife to one side. It clashed and rang against the corrugated iron wall before dropping with a soft thud to the earth floor. Jarrad looked past the man in the donkey jacket to stare at the other three facing him. One of them was a young tearaway, cropped head, perhaps early twenties and terrified: Jarrad could see it in his eyes, the half-crouched stance, the shaky legs, the knife in nerveless fingers. Jarrad raised his chin, his cold eyes fixed on those of the young man. The tearaway got the message, and dropped his knife quickly. There'd be no trouble from him, it seemed. Jarrad's glance shifted to the other two, further back in the barn, and he realised they might be a different proposition.

They were both backing away, slowly. They had been engaged in the singeing process, burning off the skin and wool, turning the carcasses into a golden brown. The blowtorches in their hands were still flaring noisily. Jarrad made an angry gesture, stepping forward. "We don't want trouble here, lads. Set them aside. We've got you nailed, so let's make it easy, hey?"

The man nearest Jarrad was in doubt; he raised the blowtorch, hesitating. He glanced at his companion, shadowed behind him, uncertain. He looked again at Jarrad, moving slowly forward, and the five men at his back. He was clearly weighing up the odds, calculating his chances. His glance swept around the barn, as though seeking a way out, but there was only the one entrance, behind the police officers. With a reluctant sigh he switched off the blowtorch.

It was when the second blowtorch flared angrily that Jarred knew they were going to have the kind of trouble he had not expected.

The officers behind him had fanned out: two of them were taking the man with the donkey jacket into custody. He wore a hangdog air, submitting quietly as he was hustled out of the barn. The young man with the cropped head held his hands wide and came forward, stumbling slightly on still shaky legs. The third man who had turned off his blowtorch seemed edgy, uncertain what to do, but was inclined to take Jarrad's advice. As two officers came forward towards him he laid aside the torch, placing it on a bench below the line of hanging carcasses.

It was the last man in the group who concerned Jarrad. They stood staring at each other like two boxers in a ring, glaring, seeking psychological dominance. Jarrad's antagonist had now backed against the wall, his shoulder colliding with one of the carcasses, which began to swing, wafting the odour of burned flesh across the barn. The milling sheep in the pens were stamping nervously, bleating their anxiety in a rising cacophony. The blowtorch was flaring noisily. Its owner was big, belligerent, thick-set; he wore bloodstained jeans and a heavy jacket, zipped up to the throat. A black woollen balaclava covered his head and face, protection against the heat of the torch. He seemed riveted to the spot, his eyes glazed but there was a jumpiness about him that Jarrad had seen before. This one would be giving them no easy ride.

"All right, pal," Jarrad gritted. "We can do this the easy way, or we can battle it out. Either way, you're gonna lose, you hear me? Now be sensible, turn that damned thing off and –"

"Back off copper!"

Jarrad stopped, something jarring with him, a memory, a tone he had heard before. The hairs at the back of his neck prickled and there was a sudden coldness in his stomach. He hesitated, his mind racing helplessly. In the pause the officer beside Jarrad shuffled uneasily, then stepped forward. The blowtorch came up, hissing, blue flames driving towards them. The officer stepped back, swearing.

There was a short silence, broken only by the heavy breathing of the men facing each other, and the shuffling, shifting, stamping of the frightened, bleating animals in the far pens. A slow rage began to rise in Chris Jarrad, a fierce anger at what was happening. He tried once again. He raised his voice, almost shouting, injecting a controlled violence into his tone.

"Look *friend*, be sensible. I know you're a hard case. I know you think you can take us. But there's no way you're walking away from this. We got your muckers; don't make things worse for yourself by doing something stupid."

Even as he spoke he knew it was a waste of time: he could see it in the man's eyes. Twenty years experience told him this was going to get nasty, but the young officer beside him was brave, inexperienced and foolhardy. Before Jarrad could stop him, hold out a warning hand, he was plunging forward. And all hell seemed to break loose.

Two of the villains were already in custody outside; the third was being led out. But just as the officer beside Jarrad launched himself, there was a commotion at the barn door, the third prisoner changing his mind, trying to make a break for it. Jarrad's companion was closing on the man in the black balaclava, it was too late to stop him and the blowtorch came up, the jet flaming yellow, searing against the face of the young officer. As Jarrad himself leaped forward, there was a high screaming, a yelling from the seemingly crazed man against the wall, an agonised wailing from the police officer as he whirled back in pain, clutching at his face. Jarrad swore, grabbed his companion's arm and thrust him away. The man with the blowtorch seized his moment and lurched away from the pens at his back, scuttling towards the barn door. As he ran, he staggered against the wall and two sheep carcasses fell, rolling along the earth floor so that he stumbled, almost fell across them, and Jarrad turned, pushing his still screaming companion aside as he plunged after the assailant.

"You stupid *bastard!*" he yelled involuntarily.

There was commotion outside in the yard. The police van that had been waiting lower down in the farm track now came roaring up through the gate, its headlights slashing across the yard, highlighting the one man struggling with the two officers, the two slaughterers already in custody huddled against the wall, a blowtorch flaring orange and blue in the night air as its owner dashed across the yard. The police van skidded into the yard, swinging crazily as it tried to cut off the man's escape, and Jarrad was almost run down himself as he careered wildly into the yard, colliding with the flame-scorched side of the van.

Jarrad was yelling at the top of his voice, meaningless words lost in the general hubbub, the screaming and shouting, the roaring of the van engine but the man with the blowtorch was running behind the parked lorries, vaulting over a low wall, charging down the track beyond. Jarrad struggled to run after him, but was impeded by the van. By the time he had dashed around behind the lorries it was to catch only a glimpse of the man with the blowtorch, the blue flame jolting crazily as the man ran down the lane. Then, suddenly, the flame was cut off. There was a thrashing sound, a crashing of bushes, and Jarrad guessed the man had left the track, was cutting through the hedge and across the open fields, down towards the valley.

Jarrad slowed, hesitated. There was still a great deal of confusion and noise behind him, a running fight as the raiding group tried to subdue the three men they had held; encouraged by the actions of the man with the blowtorch they were all making their own attempts to make a run for it. The fields ahead of him were dark, and there was now no moon. He would stand little chance of catching the man down in the wooded valley below the fell.

And behind him he could hear the continuing tumult, and a screaming still from the officer with the scorched face. Reluctantly, Jarrad turned back, retraced his steps into the yard, running across to help his companions. They milled about crazily, fighting in groups. Frustration could be relieved by a few solid punches; he delivered them to the head of the young lad who was by now all but subdued. Then, as the three villains were finally brought under control and bundled into the back of the van Jarrad assisted the wounded constable into the passenger seat, and instructed one of the other officers to remain at the barn. He detailed another to take back the car in which they had arrived. Then he climbed into the back of the van with the prisoners.

He radioed in, keeping his account brief. He gave no instructions to the van driver . He would know the first stop would have to be the hospital. Jarrad climbed into the back of the van with the three prisoners and the other officers. The van lurched, turning in the yard, bumping its way back out through the gate and down the muddy track. As they bounced their way down across ruts ground in deeply by farm vehicles Jarrad thought briefly of the man they had missed. By now he would be well away, down in the valley. There was a slow churning in

19

his stomach; sickness, frustration and panic. Back at headquarters they'd say three out of four wasn't a bad result, and they'd soon enough find out who the missing man was, and where to find him. And then there'd be time to make him pay for the mayhem he'd caused in the barn. But that didn't satisfy Chris Jarrad. The thudding in his chest continued, and a black, vengeful mist clouded his senses.

The glitter of lights from the barn suddenly disappeared behind them. The wounded officer up front in the passenger seat was sobbing, crying out occasionally in pain. One of the other two officers in the back with Jarrad stood up, one hand against the wall of the van.

"Bastards!"

He swung a fist at one of the handcuffed men. The second officer stood up with him. Bitterly, Jarrad watched as his companions began to take out their own frustration, satisfy their own pent-up hatred, taking revenge on the helpless men in their custody. He could understand their actions. One of their own had been wounded; it could easily have been them.

It had not been a good night. Jarrad had not expected trouble. Stupid, slow-witted farm labourers... When his companions eased up, he rose from his seat. It was his turn. He had his own fury to assuage.

1

Eric Ward sipped at his glass of wine as he leaned against the bar, and surveyed the function room at the Copthorne Hotel. It was the usual sort of gathering to be expected at a Law Society celebratory dinner: mainly middle-aged men, portly in their dinner jackets, ostentatiously successful, some with trophy wives, self-satisfied, red-eyed with alcohol. He had learned to go easy with the alcohol himself: too much could cause problems with his glaucoma, and in any case caution gave him the opportunity to ease back and watch some of the other lawyers make complete fools of themselves. He had never felt that he was really one of them: a previous career in the police meant that he was always regarded by them as something of an oddity, an outsider, a matter for suspicion, even though his days in the police were long behind him. Such views were exacerbated among the comfortable, more successful partners in elegant city firms in Newcastle, who could never seem to understand why he chose to stay in a one-man practice down on the Quayside, taking cases most of them would see as below their dignity to touch.

He placed his glass on the bar. As always, he wished he had not bothered to come. There were some years when he had deliberately stayed away from functions such as this; it had been his intention to do so this time, but he had been persuaded by Sharon Owen, the young barrister who worked near the Quayside at Victoria Chambers. They had become friends, but he was still a little uncertain about his feelings for her though he suspected she would like the relationship to become somewhat closer than mere friends. Or perhaps he was deluding himself, a fantasy in the aftermath of his divorce from Anne. The split had been relatively amicable, but painful nonetheless. He watched as Sharon Owen stepped out of the lobby leading into the bar, where she had been chatting with barristers from her chambers, and headed towards him.

Sharon was of medium height, with frank grey eyes and an easy smile. She was wearing a black sheath dress that hugged her figure, exposed her bare shoulders; her features were animated, her eyes sparkling, and she was clearly enjoying herself. She came forward, placing one slim hand on his arm; he was aware of several heads in the bar turning. The other lawyers would be wondering how it was that Eric Ward could be escorting Sharon Owen to the celebratory dinner. There were times when he wondered himself.

"The judge and his party have just arrived," Sharon said. "And you wouldn't believe some of the stories I've been hearing about him!"

Eric laughed. He would. Mr Justice Dawson, in whose honour the dinner was being held, had lived a somewhat chequered existence. A period in the Judge Advocates department in the Army had given him a certain liking for the more louche among his contemporaries at the Bar and it was rumoured that as a young man he had escaped through more than one window just moments before an enraged husband had arrived back home. Now retiring from the bench, his tall, lean figure was stooped and his white hair had thinned but he still possessed an active and sharp-witted mind, maintaining his reputation to the end: he was well known for making bad jokes, inappropriate witticisms, and political gaffes. He was also proud of his reputation for gallantry, and directness and fairness in his judgements.

As Eric moved aside slightly to let Sharon reach her drink he became aware that Mr Justice Dawson was entering the room with a small group of people. Peter Henderson, President of the local Law Society was one of them and he was looking a little flustered. Eric could guess what had happened: Henderson would have arranged for a private room for pre-dinner drinks, exclusive to a small coterie; he should have known better because the judge was well known for wanting to mingle with the diners in general at such functions. He regarded it as more democratic. And the women weren't restricted to staid wives.

The judge had already caught sight of Sharon Owen, he beamed and immediately made a beeline towards her, with the rest of his flustered group in tow. He had always had an eye for a pretty face. As he approached, putting out a hand to touch her elbow, he recognised Eric standing beside her and a slight shadow of surprise touched his eyes. He nodded. "Ward. How are you? Still down among the dead men?"

"Scraping a living along the river," he replied in a casual tone, and then as the judge eased Sharon away for a moment Eric for the first time realised that Anne was one of the judge's group.

His ex-wife. He had still not entirely become accustomed to thinking of her in that context. They had not met for several months now, since the decree absolute and settlement of their financial affairs, his refusal to accept more than he considered due from the marriage, and his involvement in the business that had damaged her lover's reputation. Now, their glances met and locked:

she seemed thinner about the face, and he felt there was a certain haunted look about her eyes, but that could have been just his imagination.

The judge was talking in animated fashion with Sharon, making no secret of his admiration for her appearance while Henderson ordered a gin and tonic for him and hovered uncomfortably. Anne approached Eric, with a faint smile on her lips. "Eric. I was hoping you might be here." Her glance slipped to one side. "Though I had assumed you would probably be alone."

"Really? I'm surprised to see you here with the judge."

"You forget. He was one of my father's old friends. But you've clearly not let the grass grow under your feet."

He shrugged diffidently. "Sharon Owen and I are here together, yes."

She glanced sideways. "Pretty girl."

He nodded. "And how's *your* friend?"

She knew who he was referring to: Jason Sullivan QC had been one of the reasons for the break-up of their marriage. She held his glance coolly. "He's well enough. You'll no doubt have heard he's stepped down from the board of Morcomb Enterprises, though I pressed him not to. I told him I had every confidence in him."

"*Naturally.*"

He regretted the word and the sarcasm in his tone: it was a cheap shot, and her back had stiffened. She raised a contemptuous eyebrow. "Jason has also appeared before the Benchers of his Inn. They have decided no action is warranted."

The hearing would have been in private. Eric guessed some stern words would have been spoken, because the part played by Jason Sullivan in the history of the *Sierra Nova* had been somewhat murky. Nevertheless, the QC must have talked his way out of a difficult situation it seemed, though no doubt he would be more circumspect in his future dealings outside the courtroom.

"And of course," she continued in a cool tone, "Morcomb Enterprises also came out of the whole sorry business with a clean bill of health. Jason had been conned, drawn into the dealings by unscrupulous men –"

"Poor darling."

Again he regretted the words. But as he hesitated, wishing to apologise, he felt a light touch on his arm. Sharon had escaped from Mr Justice Dawson and was standing beside him. "Ah… Sharon, I don't believe you've ever actually met my ex-wife. This is Anne."

He felt a slight tremor in her fingers; she removed her hand from his arm, as though not wishing to seem possessive. She hesitated, then held out her hand. "Mrs Ward. No, we haven't met."

"Miss Morcomb, actually," Ann replied. "I've used my maiden name professionally for years; now, I've formalised the situation. And you, of course, are the young lady who was involved in the *Sierra Nova* business."

"Peripherally, and quite innocently, I assure you," Sharon replied. "But I didn't mean to intrude…"

"No intrusion, I assure you Miss Owen," Anne replied with glacial dismissiveness, and turned back to Eric. "The reason why I wanted a quick word with you is to find out whether you've heard about Paddy Fenton, the tenant farmer on the Morcomb Estates."

"If this is private…" Sharon tried again, uneasy.

"It isn't," Anne snapped dismissively. "Eric knows Paddy from way back."

Since the beginning of Eric and Anne's marriage in fact. Paddy Fenton held the isolated acres known as

Ravenstone Farm, on the hills above the valley which formed part of the sprawling Morcomb Estates. He was from Kilkenny originally, in his forties now, stubborn, headstrong, inclined to speak his mind, and occasionally known to drink a little too much when he had something to celebrate. But he was a likeable man, and Eric had got on very well with him.

"So what's happened to him?"

"He's been arrested."

"A fight down in The George?"

Anne shook her head impatiently. "I wouldn't bother if it was just that. It's more serious. And if the charges are to be believed... Anyway, you know what he's like. Stubborn, won't take advice, even when it's well meant."

Eric knew she wasn't simply referring to Paddy Fenton when she made the comment, but he refused to rise to the bait. "What's he been up to, then?"

The master of ceremonies was calling from the doorway: it was time to move in for dinner. Anne shook her head. "I haven't time to explain now. I must get back to the judge. But I've done all I can to talk to Fenton; I think he'll listen to sense if you spoke to him. He certainly needs a lawyer. He's in bigger trouble than he seems to realise, or accept. Talk to him, Eric." She turned, moving away. "I hope you enjoy your evening, Miss Owen."

"I'm sure I shall, Miss Morcomb."

From the frosty edge in both their tones, Eric was left with the feeling that it would be unwise ever to put money on the two women ever becoming friends. He followed Sharon into the dining room to their table.

The next two hours passed pleasantly enough; the meal was well up to standard for Law Society functions, and he enjoyed Sharon's company but when coffee was served his mind was on other things as he was forced to listen to seemingly interminable reminiscences about the guest of honour from Peter Henderson, before the judge himself rose to speak. At least, the old man was witty. And somehow, Anne, seated to the judge's right, contrived never to glance in Eric's direction.

When he took Sharon home, neither of them mentioned Anne, but somehow an awkwardness had seemed to touch their relationship, and Eric refused the offer of a nightcap at her flat. She herself seemed a little relieved at the refusal.

Eric took the opportunity to visit Paddy Fenton the following Saturday morning. He drove north to the fells with somewhat mixed feelings. It was the first time he would be taking the old, familiar routes since the divorce: the distant views of the sea as he climbed the hills, the narrow roads twisting alongside bubbling streams, glimpses of the Cheviot as he ascended the moorland where buzzards circled high on the thermals, and pheasant and grouse crouched for cover in the heather, these were all well known sights to him. During the years of his marriage to Anne he had taken these narrow lanes weekly, maintaining his office on the Quayside but travelling home to Sedleigh Hall to spend weekends riding with her along craggy rock ledges, past harebell and wood sage, ancient woods of relict oak and ash, and across the sprawling meadowland where the old beech trees guarded the glittering, meandering stream that led down to the house itself. They had been good years, and there were times still when he felt unable to understand just where things had gone wrong, when the seeds of a destructive doubt had been sown, and wonder whether things might have been different if something had been said, an explanation not sought, an unwarrantable suspicion stifled. But he was unable to escape the consequences of his own personality, his stubbornness, his unwillingness to compromise, his insistence on sticking to what he regarded as important matters of principle.

They had been good years, but they were in the past. They were over.

He breasted the hill in his Celica and caught his first glimpse of Ravenstone Farm. Its sturdy stone buildings were clustered on the isolation of the craggy ridge, just below the sheltering sycamore and beech trees that had been planted years ago to protect the farm from the east winds that could come driving down over the fell in the winter. A narrow farm track led up from the main road that Eric traversed; hedged with blackthorn and whitebeam the track was deep cut, ridged with tractor ruts and Eric was forced to drive carefully as he edged his car up towards the barns. There were no sheep in the stone-walled pastures, though a small herd of cattle grazed in the home field. The acreage spread all the way down into the valley, and Paddy Fenton had been farming it as a tenant of Morcomb Estates for more than twenty years, but Eric felt it had changed in appearance: there was an air of despondency about the place, a lack of care. He noted some collapsed walls, fences needing repair, and he grunted disapproval as something thudded underneath him as the car shuddered and banged over loose rocks in the rutted lane.

The gate leading into the farmyard was closed. Eric got out, opened the gate, returned to the car and drove through, across the yard and around to the side of the house. There was no stock to be seen so he did not bother to close the gate behind him. A few chickens scratched among the ill-tended flowerbeds just outside the main entrance to the sturdy, eighteenth century stone farmhouse and the cobbled yard was unswept, littered; Eric knocked on the door and waited. In a little while he heard steps on the stone-flagged floor within. The door opened, and Paddy Fenton stood there in his shirtsleeves.

He was perhaps six feet in height, broad-shouldered, with an open, wind-tanned face. His hair was reddish in colour, thinning at the crown; his eyes were a startling blue and his features craggy, a broken nose from a bar room brawl, a scarred lip from a drunken fight. His arms were brawny, freckled, with reddish hair in abundance; a mat of chest hair showed at his throat. When he saw Eric a broad smile crossed his face and he extended his hand. "Mr Ward. 'Tis good to see you."

Eric had always known him as an affable man. There had been occasions when they had gone fishing together at weekends, years ago, and Eric had often stopped at the farm on his walks among the hills. He had sometimes come across Fenton when the farmer was rounding up his sheep on his quad bike, and he had watched the Irishman as he whistled to his sheepdog, marvelling at his control over the animal, the skills and training displayed. But he was well aware there was another side to Paddy Fenton's character: when his hot Irish blood was up and he had stowed away a few pints of beer with whisky chasers he could be belligerent, easily offended, quick with his fists. His wife Margaret kept him in check most of the time – also Irish, small, seemingly fragile but determined, she could instil fear in him with her tongue, but she never ventured into a pub with him and it was usually there that the trouble started.

"Margaret's not home at the moment," Paddy boomed, half dragging Eric into the stone-flagged corridor that led towards the farmhouse kitchen. It was untidy, dirty dishes in the sink, clutter on the old oak table itself. "Ye'll not be aware, but her sister's not been well, back in Kilkenny. They say it's cancer, so Margaret has gone back there to spend some time with her. I was there a while meself, to be sure, but I had to get back to look to the farm, you understand. So it's the lonely bachelor I am at the moment. But tell me, how's yerself?"

He gestured Eric to a chair in front of the kitchen table, pushed aside a few plates and from the cupboard above the chest of drawers set in the corner of the room he produced a bottle of Irish whiskey and two glasses. "Ye'll take a quick one with me, of course, if only because it's a while since we've had a word."

"Just the one," Eric agreed. "And life's been treating me well enough. Plenty of business."

"And that'll have taken your mind off other things," Paddy remarked as he poured two generous tots of whisky. "I saw Mrs Ward the other day –"

"Miss Morcomb again, now," Eric interrupted.

Paddy Fenton was silent for a moment. He seemed uncomfortable. "Aye, well, bad business that. I would never have thought it possible, you know."

"People change."

"They do that," Paddy Fenton agreed soberly and sipped his drink self-consciously. He thought it better to change the subject. "But what brings you up here on the hills?"

"Something Anne said to me. I met her the other

evening, at a function in Newcastle. She gave me no details, but said that you were in some kind of trouble."

Fenton grimaced. "Not as much trouble as will be faced by the villain who led me into all this!" he asserted.

"What's it all about?"

"Ah, I'm not sure you'll be wanting to hear this," Fenton suggested reluctantly. "It's all a bad misunderstanding, but if I get my hands on that bastard..."

"Tell me about it," Eric insisted.

Fenton was silent for a little while, considering the matter, then he shrugged, downed his whisky in one gulp and stood up. "Come with me and see for yourself."

Eric finished off his own drink and followed as the Irishman led the way out of the back doorway to the farmhouse, turned the corner into the yard and headed towards the long, corrugated iron barn. Over his shoulder, Fenton said, "Only put up this barn three years ago. Before all the foot and mouth troubles came. That was a bad business, I tell you. Got decimated, I did. Lost almost all my stock, apart from a few who were up there on the fell, well out of danger." He reached the barn door, dragged it open, and with his mouth twisted in distaste gestured inside.

Eric stood beside him, looking into the barn. It was empty, except for some pens at the far end of the building. But the floor was filthy with dark matted straw, and there was a sweet, sickening odour in the air, stained, rusting hooks hanging from the walls down the length of the barn, a general atmosphere of chaotic disorder.

"What on earth's been going on here?" Eric asked.

"Smokies. That's what they call them, I understand. And when I get my hands on that bastard who set me up..." Fenton's voice died away as he stood there, glaring into the barn, but Eric could sense the tension in the man, the despairing fury that surged in his veins.

"Better tell me about it," he said quietly.

"Not here. Not in this bloody slaughterhouse," Fenton replied bitterly and clanged the door shut. They made their way back to the house, and the kitchen. Paddy Fenton poured himself another stiff whisky. Eric declined the offer: one was enough.

"It all started eighteen months ago," Fenton began, glaring at the golden liquid in the glass in front of him. "There'd been the earlier trouble with BSE of course, but I had mixed stock up here at Ravenstone and I survived that well enough. But it was the foot and mouth that hit us hard, like most of the other farms around here. It was all a cock-up of course, the Ministry didn't seem to know what they were doing, there was a pall of smoke, you could see it drifting across the hills from the burning of carcasses, there were protests from some of the villagers across the valley when the Government set up a burial site because it could affect water supplies, there were stories of lorries leaking blood in the roads, I tell you it was all hell. I'm still convinced my own farm was clean, but there was a confirmed outbreak down in the valley and the bloody Ministry vets came onto my land to check out the stock and then said that since their own vehicles might be infected and had been across my land they'd have to take precautions, and cull my flocks. I had some sheep up on the top pastures, well out of the way, and they were saved, but I couldn't move them of course, and feed was scarce... I tell you it was all a bloody mess."

"You were just about wiped out," Eric said sympathetically. "I heard about it."

Fenton grunted sourly. "It was pretty general up here on the fells. There was compensation paid, of course, and some would say we all did well out of it in a sense. But there's more than a few have decided the game wasn't worth the candle, sold up and closed down. I decided to go on – it's the only thing I know – but stock prices were high, and it's been a problem. And to top it all, Margaret's sister was taken ill and I sort of took my eye off the ball, so to speak."

"What happened?"

Fenton shrugged his brawny shoulders. "I'd taken Margaret across to Kilkenny and stayed a while with her sister, then came back. But I just wasn't organised. And when I got this approach… it wasn't just that it seemed like easy money; it gave me the chance to go back again, be with Margaret. She was very close with her sister."

"Easy money?" Eric queried.

Fenton scowled, an angry light dancing in his pale blue eyes. "I was down at the livestock market, just having a chat because there wasn't much happening there, it had been a disappointing day, the market had just opened again after the disease closures, when one of the local lads – Joe Robson – came up to me. Asked me if I'd be interested in hiring out my barn for a few days. He said he knew a man who'd be willing to rent it at a good price. Of course I was interested: I had nothing to speak of in the bank other than an overdraft, and any ready cash would be useful. Ministry cheques were slow coming in, believe me. So I met this guy… this bastard, who offered me three hundred quid a day for the use of my barn. And he was hiring local labour as well, he said, but I was more interested in getting back to Kilkenny to be with Margaret. So the upshot was, I agreed."

"Did you ask this man what he wanted the barn for?" Eric asked.

Paddy Fenton hesitated. He seemed vaguely uneasy. "Course I did. It was my barn; I'd want to know that. He said he'd be herding sheep in there for slaughter. I asked him why he didn't use a licensed slaughterhouse. He told me they were too expensive because of the hygiene regulations, and it was more convenient up at Ravenstone, and it was only going to be meat for the pet food industry anyway. And you got to remember, Mr Ward, I'd about had my fill of bloody regulations right then. And," he added slowly, "like I said, the money he offered was good."

"So you agreed."

"I agreed. He paid me something in advance. I went back to Kilkenny. And then, a few days later, that's when the Gardai came around to see me. They suggested I should get back to my farm as soon as possible. And when I did, I got arrested. For being involved in the production of smokies."

"I don't understand the term," Eric admitted.

"I didn't at the time. Since then, I've been educated," Paddy Fenton said grimly. "It was what that bastard wanted to use my barn for. It seems that smokies are regarded as a delicacy among African communities. They're produced by killing sheep and then scorching the hides with a blowtorch. The guys who eat it, they believe the system sort of recreates the taste of an animal that's been roasted outside on a spit. And I'm now told it's big business. It's illegal, of course. The meat is sold uncooked and is then boiled or roasted by the consumer before eating. The inner organs such as the heart and lungs are left in –"

"The spinal cord?" Eric asked.

"The spinal cord too."

Eric began to understand. He was well aware of the raft of laws and regulations, many brought in to combat BSE, that sought to prohibit the sale of products which might contain what was described as 'specified risk material' such as the spinal cord. They could get into the human food chain if sold alongside legal meat or handled by butchers dealing with other produce.

"I been reading up on the whole business," Fenton went on. "It seems smokies are made legally in Australia, but there the skin is removed and treated before being replaced. It's different in this country. But I'm not bloody involved in all this. Like I told the coppers, all I did was to rent out my barn!"

Reluctantly, Eric said, "I don't think that defence is going to get you very far, Paddy. It's your barn, the offences were committed there… Have they arrested anyone over the matter?"

Fenton nodded, his eyes hard. "Oh, aye, they did that well enough. They caught the group doing the slaughtering in the barn; it was a police raid. They got the local lads, Joe Robson, and Mick Milburn, and a young lad called Armstrong. But it seems things got pretty nasty during the raid. There was one other guy, the one who had set it all up. He had a blowtorch. A copper got injured. Burned his face. The man who did it got away, but the coppers are really mad about the whole thing. And they're tying me into it. But my conscience is clear. I've told them my side: I had nothing to do with the whole thing."

"You rented the barn to them."

"But that's all! The rest of it, it was all set up by that

bastard who got away. He was the one who made me the offer after the meeting at the livestock market. And if I get my hands on him I'll break his bloody back." He paused, breathing hard, eyeing Eric carefully. "They released me without charge, Mr Ward, but Mrs Ward… she said I ought to get legal representation. But I'm not too happy around lawyers. No offence, but I don't think I need anyone to speak for me, I'm bloody innocent, I was just conned–"

"You'd better let me talk to a few people," Eric replied cautiously. "I think this might be more serious than you think."

2

DCI Charlie Spate was bored.

He had never regarded himself as an intellectual and some of DS Elaine Start's comments about films and books left him unamused and uncomprehending. Nor was he particularly interested in wandering around historical sites. He would have been far happier just sitting in the sunshine with a glass of wine at the restaurant in the square outside the Palace of the Popes, watching the world go by, or even at one of the numerous sidewalk cafes that lined the Rue de la Republique. But their visit to Avignon was leaving him feeling a little sour.

When the Chief Constable had informed him that Charlie was scheduled to attend an international conference on crack cocaine for three days in Avignon he had merely seen it as a welcome break from routine; when he had learned that Detective Sergeant Elaine Start was also to attend he had perked up considerably. She was a woman who intruded erotically into his dreams from time to time. The fact she was a fellow officer caused certain problems; the fact she treated him with a certain amused indifference made things even more difficult. And she was clearly aware of some of the rumours that had drifted up from the Met with him – it had not been an entirely spontaneous decision on his part to effect the transfer. It had been made clear to him down south that there was too much mud sticking for him to consider a continuation of his career in the Met, too many rumours of close dealings with villains, too many personal links with women on the streets. He had denied the truth of the rumours, argued that such contacts were necessary in the search for underworld information, but he had been forced to admit there was a little fire behind the smoke, and had moved north. But hints had filtered north with him, and Elaine Start was careful in his presence. There had been a few occasions when he thought he had detected a certain warmth, but they had come to nothing.

Yet he had the feeling that warm southern nights in the ancient citadel of Avignon might just tip a balance for both of them. He did not think that the additional presence of Assistant Chief Constable Charteris would particularly affect the issue, or the opportunity. But he had been proved wrong.

It was clear that Elaine and Jim Charteris had interests in common. On the flight out they had been chatting in animated fashion about films. The three had arrived at Avignon in the early evening. The conference was due to start the following day, in the late afternoon, so they had the opportunity to relax and do some sightseeing in the morning. At first Charlie had trailed along through the sunlit streets, agreeing that the Palace of the Popes with its huge machicolations, narrow openings and massive pointed arches was a stunning sight, but he had soon got bored looking at the wall decorations, frescoes and tapestries that adorned its interior.

They had stopped for a coffee in the Place de l'Horloge but when Charteris and Elaine had decided they wanted to walk down to the famous Pont St. Benezet, the Bridge of Avignon immortalised in the celebrated song, Charlie had had enough. He had declined, told them he'd stay on at the café outside the baroque façade of the Hotel des Monnaies, and await their return for lunch.

He watched them go, chatting amicably about dragons and eagles and pontifical legates, and he was irritated. He ordered a bottle of red wine and eyed the thronging tourists who moved into the square, climbed their way up to the Jardin du Rocher des Doms, or slumped red-faced and exhausted at the café tables. His expression was surly as he watched young couples strolling past, hand in hand; he had planned an elaborate seduction: this morning to establish a friendly basis of personal confidences, the first evening to tread lightly around the possibilities with a meal under the stars, wine, a few glasses of cognac, and then the second night, before they made their way back to Newcastle, more wine, perhaps some champagne, cognacs back in his room, or hers, and the achievement of an understanding. It might make for some difficulties back at work, later, but on the other hand maybe it would clear the air between them, remove the miasma of doubt that seemed to cloud their professional relationship. There had been several occasions when he had considered Elaine Start to be up for it; but she had a way of putting a man down...

Charlie was still sitting at the café table an hour later, when Elaine and the Assistant Chief Constable re-entered the square. Jim Charteris was in his mid-forties, Charlie guessed, a well set up, slim-hipped man who was just a shade too elegant in Charlie's view. In uniform he was immaculate; today, dressed in casual slacks, white shirt, with a blue sweater carelessly tossed over one shoulder he looked at ease, informal, and clearly getting on well socially with Elaine.

As for her, she looked good. Charlie had always admired her figure: good bosom, great legs, dark hair and sparkling eyes. She was wearing a light, figure-hugging dress that exposed some of her cleavage, and she appeared to be enjoying herself. As the two of them approached, she called out, "Hey, you seem to be getting a good start on us!"

Assistant Chief Constable Charteris raised an eyebrow, as he stood over Charlie, his shadow blocking out the sun. "I hope this doesn't mean you'll start snoring during the conference speeches, DCI."

Sourly, Charlie guessed he wouldn't have been calling Elaine by her rank, while they had been walking down there on the banks of the Rhone. He stood up, pulled out a chair. "Afternoons are not my snoozing time, sir. What'll you be having to drink?"

Charteris glanced at Elaine and shook his head. "No, I'll be getting back to the hotel. There are some papers I need to read. You two get some lunch, and I'll see you back at the conference hall by three."

He nodded to Charlie, turned, and strode off purposefully across the square and down towards the Rue de la Republique. Charlie blew out his cheeks in a relieved sigh, and poured a glass of red wine for Elaine as she sat down beside him. "I'm never comfortable when the brass are around."

Elaine chuckled throatily. "He's all right," she commented. "Almost human, in fact. He read history at university before becoming a copper. And he knows quite a lot about this place: Popes and anti-Popes, the soldiers of fortune the Popes bought off to prevent pillage, the siege of 1770 –"

"Bloody hell," Charlie grunted sarcastically, "and there was I thinking he was just an ordinary copper."

"He's an educated man," Elaine replied coolly, leaving

Charlie in no doubt that it was a description she felt would not apply to him. "And interesting to listen to. Now, are you going to surprise me by displaying hidden gourmet talents?"

"What?" Charlie asked suspiciously.

"Are you going to order lunch for us? Or – if the language is a problem – would you prefer if I did it?"

Charlie had the feeling that these few days were not going to proceed entirely according to plan.

The convention was well attended, with delegates drawn from ministries and police forces throughout Europe congregating in the reception room decorated with the arms of Pope Clement VI: a blue stripe and red roses on a silver ground. Charlie checked in behind Charteris and Elaine, collected his name badge and looked around. Almost immediately he caught sight of one familiar face: as Charteris drifted off to speak to some other senior officers an old acquaintance from the Met came up to greet Charlie. They exchanged gossip for a few moments but Charlie was aware that his ex-colleague's eyes kept straying. He was clearly interested in Elaine Start, standing at Charlie's elbow. Charlie introduced them with a degree of reluctance and quickly found himself no match for the charm of the man from the Met. Charlie's growing annoyance was ended by the return of Jim Charteris and a call that the delegates should all now take their seats in the Salle du Conclave.

The timber-vaulted, blue-carpeted auditorium was equipped with a range of electronic devices including the usual slide and movie projectors and booths for simultaneous translation into four languages. Since the proceedings were to be in English, Charteris explained, they need not have recourse to the booths.

When the delegates had all settled down into their seats there was a brief introduction from the conference chairman and then the first speaker stood up to the microphone. He had been introduced as a drugs minister from the French government; he spoke English well enough but with a heavy accent. "Crack cocaine," he announced portentously, "is spiralling out of control."

Tell me about it, Charlie thought to himself.

The aim of the conference, the speaker explained, was to address the issue of the soaring numbers of crack addicts, predominantly young men living in poor inner-city areas. The problem in France, he explained, was that most of the men concerned were young and black. "This means that some areas are more at risk of suffering the devastating impact crack cocaine can have upon individuals, families and whole communities."

Charlie was well aware of the problem: he had seen it in the Met and he had seen it more recently on Tyneside. The overspill from crack usage and dealing had led to an extraordinary level of violence, and was making a major contribution to a large proportion of gun crime.

"The supply of the drug is clearly associated," the speaker went on, "with a growing culture among young people who are attracted to the possession of a firearm in the way they think leads to power and respect..."

Charlie yawned. He was already feeling somewhat drowsy. Perhaps the bottle of red wine had not been such a good idea after all, he thought, as he caught the Assistant Chief Constable shooting a warning glance in his direction.

The second speaker was from Liverpool, a deputy chief constable who spoke of the drug that was coursing through the desolate urban landscapes that made up much of Liverpool's hinterland.

"Colourful," Elaine Start murmured, leaning slightly against Charlie's shoulder to whisper to him. He liked that.

The final speaker, before the conference delegates split up into discussion groups, was a woman who worked for a drugs information and training agency. She seemed to assume a level of ignorance among her listeners: Charlie already knew about the increased profit levels that could come from powder cocaine, about how a ten quid 'rock' could give a user two hits within a few minutes, and how crack could make the users feel agitated, paranoid and delusional. He'd met his share of them in the streets. And he was well aware that the drug could be heated up without elaborate paraphernalia – a piece of tinfoil, or a perforated soft drinks can would suffice. Charlie began to nod, heavy-eyed.

When they were allocated their discussion units Charlie was once more annoyed. Not only was he put in a separate group from Elaine, but he was also designated as its chairman. It meant he had to stay awake, and make intelligent comments on contributions made by other group delegates, control the discussion, channel it if it began to wander from the issues involved, and make notes for reporting back later. He had trouble with two delegates who began an argument about the average purity of cocaine powder; the group got sidetracked by one delegate who wanted to inject arguments about the inherent racism that suggested it was mainly a black problem, and by the time he had battled through the growth in local manufacturing agencies versus Colombian suppliers of the drug, he was feeling exhausted.

It meant that when the day's proceedings ended he was not really in the mood for a *tête-a-tête* with Elaine that evening. And besides, she seemed to be getting very friendly with the Assistant Chief Constable. He saw them in the bar, heads close together, engaged in earnest, serious discussion. Elaine was listening hard, her eyes fixed on Jim Charteris as though he were the fount of all wisdom, her ladder to promotion.

It was something he brooded about the following day, when the conference was resumed. Elaine was no longer sitting next to him, as speakers droned on about cocaine seizures and Jamaican influences in the trade, the relationship between street robberies and the rise in the use of hard drugs, and the importation of cocaine in bulk by way of container traffic and vessels from Rotterdam, Antwerp and Hamburg, to ports in the south and east of England. It was at that point he made an intervention of his own. "We've received intelligence that it's not just the south and east coast that's being targeted," he interjected. "Middlesbrough has perhaps the highest concentration of drug-related crime in the UK and it's become a distribution centre. We've had entry points set up at Whitby and Scarborough, and we're already cracking down on networks that are being established in Teesside and Tyneside."

He became aware that Assistant Chief Constable Charteris was nodding in agreement. Not that Charlie cared. He was more concerned about the fact that Charteris and Elaine seemed to be getting so chummy.

The matter came to a head that evening.

It all began very well. Charteris had wandered off and

was deep in discussions with officers of his own rank in other forces when Charlie drew Elaine to one side. "I wonder whether you might fancy getting out on the town this evening. Chance to relax. Last night before we get back to the grind and all that."

"You got a smooth tongue and a way with women, Charlie Spate," she commented ironically, but after a quick glance in the direction of the Assistant Chief Constable, she agreed.

They found a small restaurant near the Rue Rouge, so called, Elaine explained, because of the blood that had been spilled in it during the siege that ended the Moorish occupation of the city in 737. Charlie was a little uncertain about the restaurant when he noted the bloody scenes enacted on the painted walls, but Elaine seemed to approve as they settled into an intimate corner of the restaurant, and she took over the ordering: a bottle of sparkling Gaillac, oysters from Bouziques, *foie gras*, and *gigot de mer de Palavas*.

"And what the hell is this?" Charlie enquired suspiciously as he peered at the sauce accompanying the fish.

"Mixed herbs, watercress, spinach, anchovies, the yolks of hard boiled eggs, butter and spices."

"How do you know that?" Charlie asked in irritation.

She smiled. "Read it from the back of the menu."

Vengefully, Charlie ordered a bottle of Languedoc.

They were well into the meal, and had just started on the Languedoc when Elaine said, "I thought your point in the conference was well taken."

Charlie was confused. "What point?"

"When you spoke out about the problems we're facing in the north. You know, crack cocaine."

"The points of entry, you mean? Yeah, well, we always

45

keep hearing about the problems in London and Liverpool, but no one seems to pay much attention to what's going on in the north-east."

"And what do you reckon is going on?"

It was not a subject he had expected to expound upon, but Elaine was leaning forward, elbows on the table, one hand cupping her chin, her blouse falling open at the throat to give him a hint of warm flesh and if he had her attention, there was nothing wrong with that. "I reckon there's all the signs of several things happening," he suggested. "First off, if you look at the statistics, there's the increase in gun crime on Tyne and Wear. Robberies with violence, and burglaries are up – and we all know that's connected with the drugs, young tearaways wanting to feed the habit. Second, controls on the ports just aren't tough enough. It's common knowledge that Customs and Excise are just out of control – we've seen how four-year investigations have got blown because of the excise guys using unacceptable procedures. They're cowboys, those clowns, unaccountable, and they're messing the whole thing about. Someone's got to get a grip. And finally, there's the whole question of distribution. We still don't know who the major dealers are on the Tyne. I'm bloody sure, myself, that Mad Jack Tenby is involved –"

She grinned at him, a flash of even white teeth. "Old horses for courses, Charlie. I thought you'd been warned off that one. He's retired, cleaned up his act, yesterday's news. You've been told."

"I can be a stubborn bastard."

"That I believe." Her tone was not critical. He thought he even detected a hint of admiration.

"And there's talk there's a new guy working the river,"

Charlie continued. "We don't have a name yet, but there's all the signs of a turf war breaking out. Now me, I don't mind if villains cut each other up, as long as we can finger the last man standing. But it's not good for the public image, your friend Charteris would say, having guys get laid out in the alleys along the river."

She ignored his comment about the Assistant Chief Constable. She toyed with her glass thoughtfully. "Charlie, have you heard anything about a haul of cocaine going missing?"

"How do you mean?"

"A drug bust that went wrong, some time back."

"In our manor?"

She shook her head. "No. It was on Teesside."

He hesitated. He'd heard the rumours but was uncertain what credibility could be placed on them. He drained his glass, poured another, inspected the empty bottle thoughtfully. "There's been a bit of scuttlebutt, but I'm not certain… there's always rumours. I've heard there was an arrest, a boat was boarded off Whitby, a stack of stuff unloaded, and then something seems to have gone wrong. No one seems to know exactly what happened, and the villains themselves got jailed. It was a good bust. But then there was the whisper that there was some discrepancy between the amount seized and the amount declared in court. I hear some of the chat has been coming out of Durham Prison. But it's all vague, and a bit uncertain. But why do you ask?"

She hesitated, as though about to say something, then shrugged, made a dismissive gesture with her hand. "I guess it's just the conference… all this concentration on crack. And you know how we coppers like to talk shop all the time…"

Shop talk was the last thing Charlie had on his mind.

They finished their meal and walked back past the cathedral along the gently sloping road beside the park towards the green hill of the Jardin du Rocher. The night sky was clear, ablaze with stars, the air was warm and the wine in Charlie gave him a warm, satisfied feeling. He slipped his hand around Elaine's waist and she seemed to make no objection.

From the gardens the seemingly endless landscape of the Rhone valley lay at their feet, bathed in a soft moon-glow, lights twinkling on the riverbank beside the Tower of Philip the Fair, glittering in the streets of the mediaeval town of Villeneuve-Les-Avignon. They stood there for a while looking out over the glistening river and she leaned lightly against his shoulder. He had been right: the occasion, the opportunity, the surroundings, they could all be conducive to moving the professional relationship they enjoyed into something more personal. But, unusually, Charlie held off: he decided to move slowly, choose his moment to the best advantage.

They strolled past the tiny lake and the couples entwined on seats under the trees. Neither of them spoke very much; it was enough to enjoy the warm night air, the atmosphere of the glittering city. They made their way back down to the Place du Palais, stopped for a coffee and a cognac in the Rue de la Republique, returning to their hotel. They collected their keys in the lobby; while they did so, Charlie noted her room number. She was located on the third floor; his room was on the second floor. He joined her in the lift, she smiled goodnight as the lifts doors whispered shut behind him at his floor. Exultant, flushed, Charlie returned to his own room and picked up the bottle of cognac he had bought earlier in the day, in preparation. He locked his door, crossed to the lift and went up to her room.

He tapped on the door. There was a short delay before she opened it. She was clearly preparing for bed; her blouse was half unbuttoned. "Charlie?"

She stepped back as he pushed into the room, grinning, waving the bottle. "Pity to see the evening fade away without a nightcap. Where's your booze glasses?"

She frowned slightly. "I'm not sure this is a good idea."

"I can't think of a better," he argued and put down the bottle. She was facing him, dark hair loose about her face, and he reached out for the magnificence of her bosom. His left arm went around her shoulders, his right hand closed on her breast and he tried to kiss her, but as his mouth closed on hers she twisted away. "Charlie! Hold off! I said this isn't a good idea!"

He was hot. His voice had thickened as he grabbed at her again. "Aw, come on Elaine. It's been a great evening, there's only one good way to end it –"

She pushed him away violently. He staggered back and his knee struck the table. Dislodged, the bottle of cognac crashed sideways and rolled onto the carpet. Elaine Start stood staring at him angrily, and irritation mixed with desire stirred in his veins. "Don't start playing coy with me, Elaine! I've known for a hell of a time you were up for it –"

"You'd better get out, Charlie," she snapped, and her tone was cold.

He glared at her, and his alcohol-fuelled desire was turning into the kind of anger that he had experienced before, years ago in the Met. It had been one of the causes for his moving north from there, and the memory made him even angrier. "What is it, I'm not good enough for you?"

She said nothing, but her eyes were furious.

"I seen the way you been smooching up to Charteris this last two days," Charlie snarled bitterly. "Is that the deal, then? You're willing to get laid by nothing less than an Assistant Chief Constable?"

The short silence was broken only by their heavy breathing as they glared at each other. Then, slowly she stepped past him, pushing him aside; she reached down and picked up the bottle of cognac, gripped the neck between her fingers. Her voice had a ragged edge to it. "Charlie, you're a stupid, horny bastard, and I'm not the pushover you clearly think I am."

"So is Charteris turning up here later then, when you've got me out of the way?" Charlie sneered.

Slowly she raised the bottle, her eyes blazing. "It would take a hell of a lot of explaining, but if you don't get out of here Charlie, I'm going to break this bottle over your head!" He could see that she meant it. There was a short silence. His desire and his anger suddenly cooled. He put out a hand, began to stammer an apology. She cut him short.

"Get out of here Charlie! *Now!*"

He found it difficult to sleep after he returned to his room. Frustration niggled at him, mingled with the thought that he had made a fool of himself, made the kind of mistake that had caused him trouble in the past, in the old days at the Met. And there was a certain anxiety gnawing at him also: he doubted whether Elaine Start would say anything about the incident, but he could not be certain.

He went down to breakfast a little late. Elaine Start was already in the dining room, seated at a table with Assistant Chief Constable Jim Charteris. He looked up as Charlie entered the room and his expression was grim. He rose as Charlie came forward. She must have said something. Charlie felt as though there were a lead weight in his stomach.

Charteris faced him. His tone was serious. "You're going to have time just for a quick breakfast, because you're going back to Newcastle on the eleven-o-clock morning flight."

Charlie's glance slipped past Charteris to Elaine. She was staring at him, but when his glance flicked in her direction she looked away. He guessed he could expect the worst, but he was not the man to give Charteris satisfaction. "If it was about last night –" he began defensively.

"What? Last night? What are you talking about?" Charteris was frowning, confused. "I don't give a damn about last night, if you went out and had a few drinks in the town, that's your business. The main thing is you need to be on that flight. Detective Sergeant Start and I will be staying on till the close of the conference but you're wanted back at Ponteland. Immediately. You're to head up a murder enquiry."

"Murder?" Charlie repeated dully.

"A body found on a waste dump."

Charlie looked again at Elaine, as a feeling of relief drained the anxiety from his veins. She was looking at him directly now, and he knew she had guessed what had been going through his mind.

There was a challenging contempt in her eyes.

3

The Quayside practice remained busy during the next week. Eric found little time to deal with the issues surrounding the arrest of Paddy Fenton, though such enquiries as he was able to make suggested that Paddy, released without charges being made but still under investigation, would not be arraigned at an early date, pending further enquiries.

The decision surprised him but he was unable to obtain any information from the court clerk, other than that the three men arrested at Ravenstone Farm would be appearing in court on the following Thursday.

"As for your client, there is no schedule for his appearance. The prosecution have informed the court that the scope of the enquiry is to be widened. I'm afraid I can say no more than that. Is… er… is Mrs Cartwright well?"

The court clerk, a balding, middle-aged widower, had a soft spot for Eric's secretary, which had proved useful from time to time, in getting information through the back door. Eric was not above using that route when it was necessary.

He felt it would not be a bad idea to call in at the magistrates court on Thursday, to pick up some background on the Ravenstone business. Susie Cartwright was not pleased. "Mr Ward," she reproved him, "I've been asking you to complete those costings for a week now. If we don't get the bills submitted for taxing, we won't be getting any money in. And if there's no money coming in –"

"There'll be nothing to pay your salary," Eric intervened, holding up his hands in mock submission. "But have I ever let you down?"

"There's always a first time," she persisted. "And this could be it."

"This afternoon, I promise," he said and slipped out before she could make further protest. She was right, of course: that was one of the problems in a one-man practice. With just one secretary and two legal executives to cover the business there was not much scope for expansion, everyone was overworked, and money could be slow coming in. It was something that had made Anne angry: she had felt he was wasting his talents and skills. She had persuaded him to take a seat on the board of Martin and Channing, to look after her interests – while he had found the work interesting, corporate law was not really his scene, and he had been glad in due course to get away from it. Anne had never understood that he liked the kind of work he did, well away from the glamour of the big, polished offices of the large firms in the city. This was the kind of work he enjoyed, and found fulfilling: it kept him in touch with the waterfront, and the mean housing estates where he had spent so much time on the beat, as a policeman. They were real people, with real problems.

Though, he had to admit, not much money.

He took the short walk in the morning sunshine up the hill from the Quayside to the magistrates court where the preliminary hearing was to be heard. He took a seat near the back of the room: the case had attracted little interest, and there were only a few journalists present.

Two other cases were quickly dealt with as he waited: he recognised one of the accused, and was pleased he was not involved in his defence. It would be a forlorn hope, the young man would be given a community sentence, again, would be back on the streets within the hour, again, and probably breaking into premises that very night, for the frustrated police force to haul him in once more to have his wrist slapped. When the first two cases had been dealt with Eric leaned back in his seat and watched as the hearing he was interested in began; the three men came in, were arraigned and the cases against them laid out by the young solicitor acting for the prosecution. It was the kind of task Eric was very rarely called upon to do: prosecution work did not come to his office. He was known to spend almost all of his time on defences, and reliance was usually placed upon the bigger firms as far as prosecutions were concerned.

He took stock of the three men charged: Ray Armstrong, Joe Robson and Mick Milburn. They were dressed in well-worn dark suits, sullen, heads down; only the youngest, crop-haired man seemed visibly nervous. The solicitor acting for the defence made little argument against committal. Three policemen were called to give evidence against the accused, in relation to offences against health and safety regulations, in the slaughtering of animals for human consumption in premises unlicensed for that purpose.

But there was a further set of charges which caused Eric to lean forward with interest. Each of the accused was charged with obstruction, assault upon police officers and with being accessories to attempted murder. He listened as the three police officers gave evidence. The final officer was a Detective Sergeant Jarrad, thick-set, fortyish, controlled and quietly confident in manner. He had clearly been in command of the operation that night. His answers to the questions posed were brief, succinctly stated, with only occasional glances at his notebook. The prosecuting solicitor took him carefully through his evidence: the initial arrests of the three accused, the fourth waving a blowtorch, the attempt by the three men already in custody to break free, the attack upon an officer, badly injured about the face with the blowtorch.

"And the person who committed the attack upon the injured officer?"

"We are still trying to apprehend the man," Jarrad replied.

"Have the accused been helpful in the matter?"

"They have offered no assistance."

The magistrate was stony-faced when the evidence was completed.

The defence waived any rights to cross-examination. Eric agreed with the decision. The three accused would be sent to trial in any case after Jarrad's evidence, and it was sensible tactics to keep the defence powder dry. He listened as the solicitor for the prosecution summed up to the magistrate.

"While it is clear that there was no initial intention to cause injury to any person, the course of events on the night in question demonstrate that the three accused, already committed to an illegal course of action in the slaughtering of the animals in the barn, thereafter continued to act in concert, in support of the person who has yet to be apprehended. It is conceded that they themselves did not take any physical part in the attack upon the injured officer, badly burned by a blowtorch wielded by the fourth man. But that attack itself would not have been possible, nor the escape of the individual concerned been accomplished, had it not been for the actions of Armstrong, Robson and Milburn in their assault upon the other officers, in an attempt to escape from custody and arrest..."

The magistrate's features were impassive as he listened.

"The three men seized their own opportunity to attempt escape. They struck out at the policemen who had taken them into custody, knowing that the fourth member of their group was attacking one of the officers with a dangerous weapon. They diverted attention and assistance away from Detective Sergeant Jarrad and his companion, they assisted indirectly in the escape of their colleague and to that extent should be held accountable as accessories to the charge of attempted murder. The fourth man held in his hands a lethal weapon; he showed no compunction in using that weapon; he badly injured a police officer in a murderous attempt to escape apprehension; and the three persons standing here before you were aware of his actions, assisted those actions by their own reprehensible behaviour, and should be called to account for that behaviour."

The chairman of magistrates cleared his throat.

"Sergeant Jarrad has spoken of this fourth man, the one who wielded the blowtorch. Do you expect to bring him before the bench in the near future?"

"He is still the subject of police enquiries," the prosecuting solicitor replied. "It is expected that he will be apprehended in the next few days."

"Are there any other charges to be brought arising out of these events?"

"Not at the moment, sir. Enquiries are proceeding, and there may be further charges against certain other individuals, not least the occupier of the premises in which these events took place, but it is the intention of the prosecution to deal with these at another date..."

So no decision had yet been made about Paddy Fenton. Quietly, Eric rose to his feet. He needed to hear no more. The outcome was inevitable, with the solicitor acting for the prisoners reserving his defence. The magistrate would be binding the three men over for trial at an appropriate time at the Crown Court. As he turned and headed for the door he was surprised to see a familiar face among the scattering of people in the last row of seats.

Mr Justice Dawson caught his glance, raised his eyebrows and nodded. Then, to Eric's surprise he raised a hand, lifted a finger, and then jabbed it towards the door in the clear suggestion that Eric should wait for him outside the court room. Eric went out, and waited in the narrow corridor at the top of the stairs. After a brief delay, the doors of the magistrates court opened and the recently retired judge emerged. He smiled, came forward, took Eric by the elbow. "Ha, Mr Ward. Thank you for waiting. I'm surprised to see you in court. Interested in these chaps up for trial?"

"Not particularly."

"You're not representing them, of course." Dawson looked at him quizzically. "But I hear you've agreed to act for someone else who is... involved. A Mr Fenton."

"The legal grapevine always did work efficiently, Judge. Yes, I've agreed to act for Paddy Fenton, but I'm surprised no action seems to have been initiated against him as yet."

Mr Justice Dawson smiled, displaying stained teeth. He was known to be an inveterate pipe smoker. "My understanding is that the charges are being... mulled over, shall we say? The wheels of justice grind slowly, as you well know."

Eric was puzzled. "I'm surprised to see you in the court, sir. I would have thought you'd have found better things to do in your retirement than sit in on magistrates hearings."

Dawson laughed, and began to stump down the echoing stairs. "Busman's holiday, you might say. Yes, indeed, but it's surprising what harnesses await you in retirement – and how soon after retirement they are attached to your neck." He glanced quickly at his wristwatch. "Would you be free in about an hour's time, Ward? I have some people I need to see, but I would appreciate it if you could find time to join me for a drink, and a little chat. The Wig and Pen, say, in an hour?"

Eric hesitated, but the judge already seemed to have assumed his assent. He was walking out into the street, one hand raised in farewell. Puzzled, but interested, Eric thought it would be best if he accepted the invitation.

He returned down the hill to the Quayside, and took the files from Susie, standing like a guardian, thin-lipped with determination, in the doorway to his room. He settled down for a while to the files: it was a necessary task, but one he hated. "You know," he called out to Susie, "this is a waste of my time. We ought to send these things out to a costing clerk."

"I've been telling you that for months, Mr Ward."

He checked through the files and silence descended for the next fifty minutes. But she was hovering again with another armful of files when he finally rose from his desk and he was relieved to escape her stiff back and disapproving glare on the excuse that he was to meet Mr Justice Dawson.

The retired judge was already established at a table in the bar of The Wig and Pen. He waved a hand to Eric.

"I've already got a gin and tonic. What can I get for you?"

"I'll settle for a coffee, if you don't mind."

"Ha! Sensible man. Long wet lunches are only for corporate lawyers, hey? And judges on the bench, of course. Although I seem to recall you had a stint of that kind of work – corporate law, I mean – when you represented your wife on the board of Martin and Channing. I was surprised that you gave it up. Rather better class of business than the stuff you handle on Tyneside."

"It was rather a long time ago, now."

"Not so long," Dawson mused, his narrowed eyes contemplating Eric thoughtfully. "And useful experience... But you're not interested in going back to that sort of thing?"

"Not really." Eric waited as a cup of coffee was brought to him. It had a rather better flavour than he had expected; he sipped it appreciatively, then glanced at Dawson. "So retirement is not exactly a matter just of golf and sailing, sir?"

Dawson smiled thinly. "It certainly is not. Of course, there's more time for that sort of thing, but one should never just go out to pasture entirely. Decay can set swiftly in. Mental and physical. No, the fact is, I already knew before I actually retired that there'd be a few jobs the Home Office would want me to do."

"Is that why you were in the magistrates court this morning?"

Dawson's old eyes were contemplative as he regarded Eric. "Like you, I was picking up a little background. Without prejudice, of course."

Eric raised an eyebrow. "How would you be prejudiced in such a case?"

"Ah, well, that's the thing." Dawson hunched forward to lean over the table. He lowered his head confidentially. "The fact is, I've been asked to… set up an enquiry. And when I saw you there in court this morning, it occurred to me that you might be an appropriate person to assist me. In a paid position, of course."

Eric frowned. He would have no objection to working with the judge: he did not like him particularly, but he respected him for his directness, intelligence and forthright view of the justice system. But he was far from sure he would enjoy working closely with him on an enquiry – they tended to be long drawn out affairs. And he doubted whether the judge was much given to making sudden decisions. "What exactly is this enquiry about, sir?"

Dawson toyed with his glass of gin and tonic; the backs of his hands were heavily veined, marked with brown liver spots. He stared at them with a certain distaste as though he resented the reality of being old. "This hearing we attended this morning," he said heavily. "It's only the tip of a very large iceberg, you know."

Eric waited silently.

"There have been a number of similar cases in West Wales, in Scotland, Norfolk, and indeed, in a number of other isolated farming areas. We're not talking here of a small group of men who are trying to make some money by illegal means: we're actually looking at a highly organised, nationwide, internationally targeted industry."

Eric stared at him in surprise. "There's been little publicity about this."

Dawson smiled cynically. "The media enjoy big stories, like murders, and terrorism, and the sexually deviant predilections of media personalities. They've tended to let slip past them sheep-killing, and a trade in possibly diseased animals."

"But you said *nationwide*," Eric pressed.

The judge nodded emphatically. "Let's consider some economic issues. The agricultural community has recently staggered out of two traumatic periods: the first was the discovery of BSE and the consequent banning by overseas countries of beef products from England and Wales; the second was the advent of a foot and mouth epidemic which most experts now, with the benefit of hindsight, would agree was very badly handled. But the result of the epidemic was that a sheep was worth at market as little as one pound at one stage. That crippled many hill farmers; we know that many bankruptcies and suicides followed. The price now has risen to maybe ten or fifteen pounds per animal, but too late to help many subsistence farmers, like the ones we find up here on the Northumberland hills. Many have had to seek other forms of employment. Those three men in the barn – Armstrong, Milburn, Robson – were slaughtering sheep and then scorching them. Do you have any idea what those scorched carcasses would be worth?"

"You're going to tell me considerably more than fifteen pounds," Eric guessed.

Dawson nodded, and sipped at his drink. "Rather more than a hundred pounds, I understand. They're called 'smokies', these carcasses, and they're destined for markets in various cities in the UK and overseas."

Eric was silent for a little while. "Those three men this morning, they wouldn't be making a great deal out of the activity."

were on the glass he twirled between his fingers. At last he looked up, his glance cool and cynical. "And why would that be, Mr Ward?"

"It would hardly be ethical."

A thin smile touched Dawson's lips. "Ethical, hey? Client's privilege, is that it? I was warned that it's an argument you might raise. But we exist in a real world, Mr Ward, peopled by criminals who will take every advantage of our weakness, both in system and professional attitude. We are looking at violent, dangerous people who are threatening health, and who are not averse to putting a blowtorch into a policeman's face. Did that ever happen to you when you were on the beat, Ward? Don't you remember the days when you faced violent desperate men in dark alleys? Did conscience stand in the way in those days? Are ethics to stand in the way of justice?"

"I'm surprised to hear a man who has been a judge talk that way," Eric replied.

"Maybe I saw too much injustice on the bench," Dawson snapped testily. "Maybe I found myself struggling against the bonds of procedure. I now have a chance to right a few injustices."

Eric shook his head slowly. "That's a matter for your conscience, sir. For me… I've already agreed to defend Paddy Fenton. There's no way I could contemplate using him in the manner you describe. I'm afraid you'll have to find someone else."

Dawson wrinkled his nose, and snorted. "So you'd rather bury your head in the muddy slime of the waterfront, and consort with the low life in the back alleys. Anne warned me how you were, and there's been talk among the legal firms… But you have the right to refuse. Still, there's one thing you need to know. If you report

"Fifty pounds a day, it seems," the retired judge suggested.

"It was stated in court that there were two hundred or more sheep in that barn up at Ravenstone. But at the prices you've mentioned –"

"It becomes an activity that criminal gangs become interested in. It's more lucrative and less hazardous than dealing in drugs. And the problem is, while the police have been able to arrest a few farmers and the men they employ, they're striking at the wrong end of the business. It's the heads of the Gorgon they want to attack, and they're getting little or no assistance from the farmers on the one hand, or the butchers who stock this dangerous product, on the other."

"I can hardly credit that it's such a major problem."

"My appointment tells you that it is," the judge averred coldly, as though offended by Eric's doubts. "Most of these carcasses find their way to markets in London. The local authorities down there are carrying out several raids each month on premises in such locations as Electric Avenue in Brixton, and the Ridley Road market in Hackney. We have information that suggests a considerable number of shops are handling hundreds of these scorched carcasses each week. Last June, for instance, more than a hundred carcasses were seized in one raid alone in Ridley Road. Vans have been tracked delivering to numerous shops in north London."

"The butchers were prosecuted?"

Dawson nodded. "They were, but they refused to say who makes the deliveries. They just say that the carcasses arrive on a van in the middle of the night. They pay cash, it's always a different driver, they ask no questions and they make a considerable profit themselves. When they're caught, they receive a small fine and that's it. They retain their profits… and it seems some of them are too frightened to talk, anyway. It's all developing into big, well organised business, Mr Ward."

Eric nodded. "I see what you mean. So what exactly is to be your involvement in all this?"

Dawson finished his drink, glanced towards the bar and raised a hand, signalling to the barman for a refill. As he waited for the drink to be brought to the table, he said, "The Government has become concerned. Environmental officers are frustrated that the courts don't seem to fine the traders enough, and they've been calling for a more centralised approach. The problem is growing, and spreading: there's good evidence to suggest that smokies are now being produced in East Anglia, Wales and Scotland."

"And now the north east."

"Exactly. And the carcasses have started appearing in markets in Birmingham and Manchester recently, as well as London. The Government wants to stop it all before it gets completely out of hand. But first, it wants to get all the facts. Consequently, it's set up an enquiry and seconded staff from the Food Standards Agency. I'm to be responsible as chairman to establish a centrally co-ordinated effort. I've got a few civil servants in tow. But I need a small team of lawyers also. It occurred to me you might be interested in working with me."

"Why do you think I would be useful?"

Dawson waited for a moment as the gin and tonic was placed in front of him. He nodded his appreciation to the waiter and then he frowned thoughtfully. "Because of your background, and your contacts. We don't have people down south who can pick up the kind of information you might have access to. The trade is too well organised down there, mouths have been closed effectively, butchers are disinclined to talk. In Northumberland, this is the first instance we've come across of the activity. There'll be other cases, we're certain. But we have the chance to break into the system as it's being established up here – and then, once we have the information, we can advise other authorities on how we can stop this dangerous activity."

"You still haven't really explained –"

"You're an ex-policeman. You know the back alleys. You know the people along the Tyne, in a way the usual run of lawyer does not. You have contacts in the county, through Morcomb Estates. You can talk to farmers and dealers, middlemen and villains. And through your practice, you've made extensive links with what may be described as the underworld along the river. You have access to information that's denied official authority. And… you are to represent this farmer Fenton, from Ravenstone."

It was now that Eric understood completely. "If I joined your enquiry team, you would expect me to… persuade Fenton to give us information."

Dawson smiled thinly, and sipped his drink with evident enjoyment. "It would give us a start. That would be one of the advantages we might enjoy if you were to join the enquiry team."

"What if Fenton knows nothing?"

"We are fairly confident that is not the case, and that you would be able to extract relevant and useful information from him."

"But you know I couldn't do that," Eric said quietly.

Mr Justice Dawson was silent for a little while; his eyes

"Fifty pounds a day, it seems," the retired judge suggested.

"It was stated in court that there were two hundred or more sheep in that barn up at Ravenstone. But at the prices you've mentioned –"

"It becomes an activity that criminal gangs become interested in. It's more lucrative and less hazardous than dealing in drugs. And the problem is, while the police have been able to arrest a few farmers and the men they employ, they're striking at the wrong end of the business. It's the heads of the Gorgon they want to attack, and they're getting little or no assistance from the farmers on the one hand, or the butchers who stock this dangerous product, on the other."

"I can hardly credit that it's such a major problem."

"My appointment tells you that it is," the judge averred coldly, as though offended by Eric's doubts. "Most of these carcasses find their way to markets in London. The local authorities down there are carrying out several raids each month on premises in such locations as Electric Avenue in Brixton, and the Ridley Road market in Hackney. We have information that suggests a considerable number of shops are handling hundreds of these scorched carcasses each week. Last June, for instance, more than a hundred carcasses were seized in one raid alone in Ridley Road. Vans have been tracked delivering to numerous shops in north London."

"The butchers were prosecuted?"

Dawson nodded. "They were, but they refused to say who makes the deliveries. They just say that the carcasses arrive on a van in the middle of the night. They pay cash, it's always a different driver, they ask no questions and they make a considerable profit themselves. When they're caught, they receive a small fine and that's it. They retain their profits... and it seems some of them are too frightened to talk, anyway. It's all developing into big, well organised business, Mr Ward."

Eric nodded. "I see what you mean. So what exactly is to be your involvement in all this?"

Dawson finished his drink, glanced towards the bar and raised a hand, signalling to the barman for a refill. As he waited for the drink to be brought to the table, he said, "The Government has become concerned. Environmental officers are frustrated that the courts don't seem to fine the traders enough, and they've been calling for a more centralised approach. The problem is growing, and spreading: there's good evidence to suggest that smokies are now being produced in East Anglia, Wales and Scotland."

"And now the north east."

"Exactly. And the carcasses have started appearing in markets in Birmingham and Manchester recently, as well as London. The Government wants to stop it all before it gets completely out of hand. But first, it wants to get all the facts. Consequently, it's set up an enquiry and seconded staff from the Food Standards Agency. I'm to be responsible as chairman to establish a centrally co-ordinated effort. I've got a few civil servants in tow. But I need a small team of lawyers also. It occurred to me you might be interested in working with me."

"Why do you think I would be useful?"

Dawson waited for a moment as the gin and tonic was placed in front of him. He nodded his appreciation to the waiter and then he frowned thoughtfully. "Because of your background, and your contacts. We don't have people down south who can pick up the kind of information

64

you might have access to. The trade is too well organised down there, mouths have been closed effectively, butchers are disinclined to talk. In Northumberland, this is the first instance we've come across of the activity. There'll be other cases, we're certain. But we have the chance to break into the system as it's being established up here – and then, once we have the information, we can advise other authorities on how we can stop this dangerous activity."

"You still haven't really explained –"

"You're an ex-policeman. You know the back alleys. You know the people along the Tyne, in a way the usual run of lawyer does not. You have contacts in the county, through Morcomb Estates. You can talk to farmers and dealers, middlemen and villains. And through your practice, you've made extensive links with what may be described as the underworld along the river. You have access to information that's denied official authority. And… you are to represent this farmer Fenton, from Ravenstone."

It was now that Eric understood completely. "If I joined your enquiry team, you would expect me to… persuade Fenton to give us information."

Dawson smiled thinly, and sipped his drink with evident enjoyment. "It would give us a start. That would be one of the advantages we might enjoy if you were to join the enquiry team."

"What if Fenton knows nothing?"

"We are fairly confident that is not the case, and that you would be able to extract relevant and useful information from him."

"But you know I couldn't do that," Eric said quietly.

Mr Justice Dawson was silent for a little while; his eyes

were on the glass he twirled between his fingers. At last he looked up, his glance cool and cynical. "And why would that be, Mr Ward?"

"It would hardly be ethical."

A thin smile touched Dawson's lips. "Ethical, hey? Client's privilege, is that it? I was warned that it's an argument you might raise. But we exist in a real world, Mr Ward, peopled by criminals who will take every advantage of our weakness, both in system and professional attitude. We are looking at violent, dangerous people who are threatening health, and who are not averse to putting a blowtorch into a policeman's face. Did that ever happen to you when you were on the beat, Ward? Don't you remember the days when you faced violent desperate men in dark alleys? Did conscience stand in the way in those days? Are ethics to stand in the way of justice?"

"I'm surprised to hear a man who has been a judge talk that way," Eric replied.

"Maybe I saw too much injustice on the bench," Dawson snapped testily. "Maybe I found myself struggling against the bonds of procedure. I now have a chance to right a few injustices."

Eric shook his head slowly. "That's a matter for your conscience, sir. For me... I've already agreed to defend Paddy Fenton. There's no way I could contemplate using him in the manner you describe. I'm afraid you'll have to find someone else."

Dawson wrinkled his nose, and snorted. "So you'd rather bury your head in the muddy slime of the waterfront, and consort with the low life in the back alleys. Anne warned me how you were, and there's been talk among the legal firms... But you have the right to refuse. Still, there's one thing you need to know. If you report this conversation, I'll deny it ever took place. And you can be certain I'm the person who will be believed. After all," he sneered, "my reputation is rather cleaner than yours, is it not?"

It was an offensive remark, and Eric resented the comment. He finished his coffee, and rose to leave. He looked down at the retired judge; his tone was cool. "I wish you well in your enquiry, sir," he said. "I regret I cannot help you."

When he returned to his office he spoke curtly to Susie Cartwright. "Get hold of Paddy Fenton. I want to talk to him. Right away."

4

There was the smell of decay in the air, sweet and rotting under the sun.

The waste disposal site was located at the side of a hill which had seen extensive quarrying over the previous hundred years. Where the side of the mountain had been gouged out to provide building materials the rock lay exposed, stark and bare of vegetation. In front of the rock cliff was an excavated area which for the last twenty years, since the closure of the quarry, had been used for the dumping of household garbage, unwanted furniture, garden waste and other discarded materials.

The area of the rubbish dump was approached by a metalled track which had now been sealed off, to the annoyance of various car and lorry drivers who continued to arrive from time to time during the day at the site to unload their rubbish. The most recent mound of garbage, old tyres, rotting vegetable materials in plastic bags, boxes, and miscellaneous items of household waste was now being worked over by men and women in rubber boots, white overalls, hoods and face masks. They were displaying no great enthusiasm for the task, unlike the raucous, clattering group of gulls wheeling above their heads, excited by the activity and the revelation of further food supplies. Several police cars were parked along the tarmac track. DCI Charlie Spate, recently returned from Avignon, sat in one of them, watching the activity with a gloomy expression.

"When did the forensic team take away the body?" he asked despondently.

"About three hours ago, guv," explained the young constable beside him in the driving seat. "The whole area has been photographed, of course, and the lads have all been warned not to do any unnecessary trampling about. But it was thought best we ought to turn over the surrounding area, in case anything else was found."

Fat chance, Charlie thought, in view of the amount of rubbish displayed and the desultory manner in which the squad of searchers approached it. He did not really blame them, however, in view of the stench arising from the mound. "How exactly did the body come to light?"

The constable gestured towards an earth-moving vehicle standing to one side of the cordoned off area of search. "The site manager reckoned it was time to shove that mound there over towards the ditch, to make more room for the weekend dumping. He got a driver to use that JCB over there. Lorries bring the stuff in, it gets piled up into mounds and then the mounds, they all get flattened out in due course. Won't be too long though before the whole quarry gets filled up, I reckon."

"And the body?" Charlie reminded him.

"Ha, well, the driver of the JCB had only just started shifting the rubbish when he thought he saw something odd. It was just a rolled-up carpet, but there seemed to be an arm sticking out of it. He stopped, got out, took a quick look, puked and then legged it up to the manager's office in that shed there. They phoned us straight away after that."

"The body was wrapped in the carpet?"

"That's right, guv."

"You said the driver saw an arm."

"That's right, just the arm. Looks as though the hand had been severed at the wrist. Probably by the JCB, when

70

it was moving the carpet. That's one of the things we've been looking for. Two hands better than one, hey, sir?"

Charlie was in no mood for macabre jokes. "All right, I've seen enough. Let's get away from here."

"Where to, boss?"

Charlie hated being called 'boss'. He scowled at his youthful companion. "Forensic laboratories. I'd better have a chat with the experts."

While the police constable drove the car towards the forensic laboratories at Gosforth Charlie remained silent beside him. He found it difficult to concentrate on the job in hand: his mind kept drifting away, sidetracked by recent events. He was still in a mood of uneasy depression. He had made a fool of himself with Elaine Start but it wasn't merely that he was embarrassed by the realisation: he was still irritated by the thought that she seemed to have preferred the company of the Assistant Chief Constable to his. He refused to accept the idea that he was in any way jealous, because he had no grounds for such an emotion, and yet the feeling gnawed constantly at him, always at the back of his mind, recurring unbidden, leading to a sourness of mood.

The police liaison officer was waiting for him in a small office just inside the main door of the laboratories. He told him that Dr Dickson was lecturing at the university, but was expected back within the next half hour. Meanwhile, he suggested Charlie might like a cup of coffee.

"Yeah, that'll do nicely."

The liaison officer vanished down the corridor and Charlie sat down, stared gloomily out of the window. He disliked the labs: the whiff of formaldehyde was unpleasant, the atmosphere was odd, and he found the flippancy of the white-coated assistants working in the pathology laboratories difficult to accept. He knew it was a defensive measure on their part, but it still irritated him.

Dr Dickson arrived just as he was finishing his coffee. The liaison officer introduced them, and Dickson waved him through to an office at the end of the corridor. Charlie sat down as Dickson removed his topcoat: he was relatively new to this job, in his late thirties, short, balding, broad-shouldered, broken-nosed, a recent arrival from Cardiff. As he sat down behind his desk he rolled his head on his shoulders, grimacing as he did so. There was a clicking sound.

"Ever play rugby?"

"No."

Dickson rubbed his thick neck. "Front row. Foolish, but you know how it is when you're a lad." His Welsh accent had been massaged but remained obvious. "All the pressure from those big buggers behind you in the scrum. Bound to have an effect in later life. Here on the neck muscles, and the spine. You'd think a doctor would know better, hey?"

"I've just been up to the waste disposal site," Charlie said.

"Oh, straight to business, is it?" Dickson commented. "All right, what do you want to know?"

"What *you* know," Charlie suggested.

Dickson had vague blue eyes. He leaned back in his chair and rolled them thoughtfully. "Well, that's not a lot. Bit early, see. But, what have we got? Cadaver. Male. Late twenties, maybe. Caucasian. User. Left hand missing. Probably cut off by the mechanical shovel that disturbed the body. Right hand intact. Possible to get prints from it. Dead a few days, it seems, but can't be precise about that just yet."

"Cause of death?"

Dickson wrinkled his nose. "Ah, well, there you are again. His face is a mess. Beaten badly, features severely disarranged. Not by the JCB. More like a club of some sorts. But he wasn't beaten to death. My colleagues and I, we are all agreed that the injuries were sustained *post mortem*."

Charlie frowned. "He was beaten after he was dead? Why the hell would someone do that?"

"I'm a pathologist, boy, not a psychiatrist. Or a copper for that matter. Not my job to guess. Just deal in facts, we do. But if I *was* to hazard a guess, maybe it was done so he wouldn't be easily recognised."

"Though it must have been hoped the body wouldn't be found at all, with it being rolled up in a carpet and dumped on a waste disposal site."

"What we hope for doesn't always come about," Dickson commented sententiously. "Now me, I always hoped to do better than Cardiff Meds second fifteen. But there you are, isn't it? We're still looking at the carpet of course. See what we can see."

Charlie eyed the pathologist quietly for a few moments. "So, when can I expect your report?"

"Hey, got a lot on at the moment, boy, so can't give you any promises, but I suppose I can give you a rundown of what we got so far." Dickson leaned back in his chair, folded his hands over what was developing into a beer belly, as far as Charlie could see. "Clearly, the man concerned did not die at the waste disposal site. He died, or was killed, somewhere else – presumably in a house somewhere – with a carpet available to roll him up in. Old carpet, well worn, not in a good state of repair. Kind you might find in a lodging house, and not a very expensive one at that."

For someone who wasn't employed to guess, Charlie considered sourly, Dickson wasn't averse to offering opinions.

"From the state of his arms, veins well punctured, he was clearly a pretty heavy user, mainliner, but we're still doing various analyses and have no clear information yet about what actually killed him. Of course, it might not even have been murder –"

"With him being rolled up that way, and dumped?" Charlie contended in disbelief.

Dickson exposed even, white teeth in a wistful smile. Then he destroyed the illusion by lifting his front teeth on their plate, with a thoughtful tongue. He inspected them on one finger. "Head butt, that was, against Ponty..." He replaced his dental plate with a sucking sound. "Maybe his body was just an embarrassment," he suggested. "In any case, we got all sort of tests going on down at the university labs, useful practice for the post-graduate students, stomach contents, all that sort of stuff, and it'll all be in the report. You'll get it in a few days. Now then, you want to see photographs of the body?"

Reluctantly Charlie rose, and nodded. He wasn't exactly keen to view the corpse down at the mortuary, but it was a duty he had to accept. Tomorrow. For the moment, photographs would do. He followed Dickson down the corridor into the laboratories: from a desk underneath a shelf loaded with lever arch files the pathologist picked up a sheaf of prints. "Here they are. Can't make much of the face, can we?"

It had been reduced to a pulped mess. Charlie scanned the other prints: a pale, lean-muscled body, mass of chest hair, close-up of the inside of the arms, marks of syringes, stump of the left arm, hand missing.

"The marks inside the arms are not recent," Dickson mused. "My guess is this character would have been on heroin, but had weaned himself off, maybe turned to freebasing?" He glanced at Charlie. "You know, crack. Dissolving cocaine powder in water and heating it with a chemical agent like baking soda to free it from the salt. Make it more potent. I understand that the average purity of crack is usually about eighty per cent, against the fifty per cent of cocaine powder. Cheaper, and more effective, the effects more intense and immediate –"

"Yeah, I was hearing all about it at a conference this week," Charlie intervened in a bored voice. "Okay, so we got a crack user who's had his face bashed in, rolled up in a carpet, dumped on a waste disposal site and you don't yet know what was the cause of death. If you can get on with that, and let me have all the details you can, I'll get on with *my* job. The first thing I got to do is try to find out who the hell the dead man was."

Dickson rolled his eyes. "Oh, I know who he was."

"What?"

"His name was Terence Charlton."

"How the hell do you know that?"

Dickson chuckled throatily, and massaged his neck with his left hand. "No great deduction necessary. We found a credit card in his shirt pocket. There was the name. Ran a forensic check on the card itself: he'd been using it to cut cocaine at some stage. Traces on the edge of the card. Minute, of course."

"Why didn't you tell me this before?" Charlie snarled angrily.

"About the identity? I'm no mind reader, boy. You didn't ask."

The meeting later in the Incident Room had been brief and stormy. Charlie had made it perfectly clear how he felt about the matter. He had stamped up and down in front of the team, haranguing them on their carelessness. It was bad enough that they had failed to find the credit card in the shirt pocket of the corpse; for them to allow an outsider, an amateur to find it was even worse. Pathologists weren't supposed to do basic detective work; that was for coppers. He was unimpressed when one of the team raised a hand, suggested that they could hardly be expected to search the body when they'd been told to wait until the forensic team arrived. Charlie glared at him: he decided the man could go back on the waste disposal shift again.

"I'm running this bloody show," he had snarled, "and you've all got off to a bad start. Things had better get shaped up. We don't have a cause of death yet but we have to treat this as murder until we know better, and we have to find out all we can about this guy Charlton and we have to do it fast. So I want to know everything, including the people he hung around with! And I want it done as if your arses were on fire. Any more cock-ups like this last one, and I'll hang the bloody lot of you out to dry."

He caught one of the men smiling at the mixed metaphors, and he too was assigned back to the dump.

Charlie had found it necessary, in his disgust, to seek liquid solace in the Mason's Arms in the village at Ponteland. It wasn't a pub he normally frequented: it was too near to headquarters, and tended to be patronised by the horse-riding fraternity, and Proctor and Gamble executives living in nearby Darras Hall. But he still seethed with anger at having been humiliated by the pathologist, and he was also annoyed that Elaine Start had not been present at the meeting in the incident room.

He had stopped her in the corridor a little while later.

"Glad to see you got back safely from Avignon," he grated sarcastically. "Pity you couldn't find time to attend my briefing."

She had looked at him coolly. "I had another meeting to attend."

"With Assistant Chief Constable Charteris, I suppose?"

She made no reply, but there was a hint of anger in her eyes.

"Anyway, you'd better call in at my room later," he continued, "so I can assign you to –"

"Sorry about that," she interrupted. "I'm not sure I'm going to be assigned to your investigation. I won't know until later today, when Mr Charteris has talked to the Chief Constable, but –" She stopped at the look on Charlie's face. "What?"

"This is a murder investigation! I need all the officers I can get."

"It's not the only enquiry we have running, and I'm under orders to report to the Chief Constable. If you have trouble with that, talk to him, not me!" Then she turned, and walked away from him.

Charlie headed for the Mason's Arms.

He was leaning on the bar, well into his second pint of Newcastle Brown Ale when he became aware of someone standing next to him. He glanced sideways. "Didn't know you drank in here," he muttered.

Detective Sergeant Chris Jarrad shook his head. "I don't. But I saw you headed this way, so thought maybe I could join you. Ready for another?"

Charlie was uncertain whether he really wanted another. He stared at Chris Jarrad. The man was relatively new to the force: tall, broad-shouldered, lantern-jawed, about forty years of age, he had kept pretty much to himself since his arrival in Northumberland. A bit of a loner by all accounts, but well-experienced, committed, reliable and steady, with a hint of cynicism about his role in life. Not unlike Charlie himself in many ways. Charlie hesitated, then drained his glass, pushed it in Jarrad's direction.

"Aye, why not? What made you think I might appreciate company?" he grunted.

"It wasn't that. Just felt it would give me the chance to have a word with you. I heard that there was a bit of trouble in your team."

"Trouble! Incompetent bastards."

"We can all make mistakes," Jarrad commented reasonably, and ordered the drinks. "Take my own case, for instance. I made a bad mistake up at that farm, not expecting that thug to come at us with a bloody blowtorch."

"Ah. I heard. The smokies enquiry. How's the constable?"

"He's still on sick leave. My own guess is he won't come back. Not sure I would want to, after getting my face scorched that way. Not sure I even want to be in the force now, for that matter. After twenty years or so, you get disillusioned." His cool grey eyes flickered sideways at Charlie. "But you soldier on."

There was an odd note in Jarrad's voice, and Charlie glanced at him curiously. "I know how you feel. But... well, then something turns up, you get on a high again, and it seems worthwhile."

"If you say so." Jarrad passed a pint to Charlie and sipped at his own. "But the longer things go on, and we have to pick up the mucky pieces the public throw at us, well, I sometimes wonder whether it's worth it. And what do we get at the end of it? A paltry pension that you can barely live on. While everyone else has been climbing past you… Still, what the hell! So, you think your new enquiry is going to give you a high?"

"Who the hell can tell? It's certainly started badly. And how is your case going? The smokies thing."

Jarrad shrugged, then shook his head. "Stalled, really. Couple of weeks now and we don't seem to be getting any further forward. Crown Prosecution Service are still haggling on about the farmer whose barn we raided: Paddy Fenton. I been pressing the guys we pulled in, but they're saying nothing, on legal advice. Bloody lawyers."

Charlie Spate grunted approval of the disgust in Jarrad's tone. He held his own views about lawyers. An unnecessary evil. "So you're bogged down."

"More or less." Jarrad hesitated. He turned almost casually to face Charlie. "But this case of yours… the body in the carpet."

"Yeah?"

"I hear on the grapevine the man's already been identified."

"By the bloody pathologist, not by one of our own people! Can you believe it? Hell, a credit card in a shirt pocket and they missed it!"

"A Terry Charlton, I understand."

Charlie took a long pull at his beer. He nodded, wiped a finger along the wetness on his upper lip. Jarrad's tone was almost too casual. He glanced at him, frowning. "So?"

Jarrad was staring at his own glass of beer. "I've come across the name myself."

"In what context?"

"The smokies."

"Talk to me."

Jarrad took a deep breath. "That night at the barn, there were four men. We took two into custody, and the third was giving up when this last bloody madman in the balaclava started swinging his blowtorch. The others tried to take advantage of the confusion, but we held on to them. The guy with the torch, well, he got away, and ever since I been pressing the three we got – Armstrong, Robson and Milburn – to lead me to their mucker. But they're staying *shtumm*. I think they're scared, or maybe they're ignorant, but I don't know… Thing is, there's been a few whispers I picked up…"

"And?"

Jarrad hesitated. "Like I said, the smokies enquiry has stalled for the time being. We're still trying to get our hands on the guy with the blowtorch. But the whispers tell me a guy named Terry Charlton has been involved with the smokies trade, among other things. I thought it might be useful if you and I, we could sort of trade information, maybe you could have a chat with the three we're holding. Maybe I could pick up what you got, and see what comes out…"

"Just what's this about?" Charlie asked suspiciously.

Jarrad hesitated. "Let me put it like this. I'm looking for a man who wielded a blowtorch. You got a cadaver who used to be called Terry Charlton. What if you already got what I been looking for?"

"You think maybe Charlton was the villain who scarred the constable?"

"I'd like to be certain," Jarrad said carefully, "if it was him. And if it was, well, I can call off the search I got going, and maybe a joint enquiry between us could put the finger on whoever killed Terry Charlton."

"You're suggesting we run in harness?"

"You got a problem with that?" Chris Jarrad queried.

Charlie Spate looked at him. There was a grimness about the detective sergeant's jaw, a hardness in his eyes that suggested to Charlie that Chris Jarrad had an axe to grind. About what, Charlie couldn't guess. Maybe it was something to do with his previous job in Teesside. Charlie could relate to that. He'd had his own problems in the Met, before heading north.

"No," he said thoughtfully, reaching for his pint. "No, I got no problem with that."

5

Susie Cartwright eventually told Eric that it was a waste of her time trying to get hold of Paddy Fenton. Either he was not at Ravenstone Farm, or he was simply ignoring the shrilling of his telephone. There was another possibility, Eric guessed: he might have returned to Ireland, to be with his wife and sister-in-law. With some hesitation, he rang Anne at Sedleigh Hall. He told her he had decided to represent Fenton, but was unable to get in touch with him.

"As far as I'm aware," she replied, "he's still at the farm. No, I don't think he's gone to join his wife."

Eric decided, later in the week, that he should go up to Ravenstone himself, to see if he could find his client.

When he arrived at the farm it seemed deserted. The door to the farmhouse was locked, the barn was empty, but Paddy Fenton's old Land Rover was parked in the littered yard. Eric walked around the house, and looked out across the fields. Somewhere in the distance he could hear a man shouting, the barking of a dog, sharp in the clear air. He went back to his car and drove down the track, out into the main road and up onto the fell. As he breasted the rise he slowed, scanning the fields. At last he caught sight of his quarry: a small flock of sheep were being worked in the distance, the border collie whipping along the fringe of the field, and the man he was looking for standing, whistling, calling instructions to the dog.

Eric got out of the car and climbed up on the gate. He waved, and called. After a few moments Paddy Fenton caught sight of him and waved back. Then, with a certain hesitation he pointed back towards the farmhouse.

"I'll be with you in a little while."

His voice seemed thin and reedy, tossed in the breeze, fading in the echoing fell behind him.

Eric went back to his car, returned to the farmhouse. He parked in the yard and waited. He turned on the car radio: it was time for the local news. The leading item stated that the police had announced a breakthrough in their investigation into the death of the man recently found on a waste disposal site. They confidently expected to be making an arrest soon.

Eric heard the rumbling of a quad bike crossing the field behind him. He looked back: Paddy Fenton was trundling up to the gate, the sheepdog crouched behind him, quivering with pleasurable excitement. He clearly enjoyed the ride. When Paddy opened the gate the dog leapt down and raced towards Eric's car. He seemed friendly. His master was surly.

"Mr Ward," he said as he came up to Eric. "Didn't expect to see you up here."

"You've not been answering your phone, Paddy."

"No one I want to hear from."

"Not even your wife?"

"She uses my mobile." He hesitated, squinted uncertainly at Eric and then jerked his head. "Come on inside the house."

He led the way across the yard, unlocked the farmhouse door, led Eric into the kitchen. He slumped down into a chair beside the kitchen table. He seemed edgy, lines of weariness or anxiety marking his features. "So what brings you up here, Mr Ward? You got any news about the case? I've heard nothing."

He was unlikely to, if he refused to answer his phone, Eric thought. He looked carefully at the farmer. He gained the impression that Fenton had lost weight; there was an air of depression about him. He seemed careworn, unlooked after. "How are things in Ireland?" Eric asked.

"She's sinking. It'll be over soon for the sister-in-law." Paddy Fenton passed a grimy hand over his face, his fingers rasping against stubble. "Then my wife can come back and maybe things can get back to normal. At least..." He fell silent, remembering that there were other issues to be faced.

"Paddy, I need to ask you a few things. About that police raid here at the farm. I'm not quite sure what's going on, but it seems they're still in the process of formulating charges against you. Have you had any approaches you haven't told me about?"

"Approaches? I don't know what you mean."

"Have the police – or any other authorities – put any pressure on you?"

"To do what?" Fenton asked almost truculently.

Eric hesitated. "I've reason to believe this thing you got involved in, well, it's pretty serious. It's bigger than I had understood. And there's a view that you probably know more than you're telling at the moment. I need to know if that's true Paddy. If I'm to act in your best interests, I need to know everything you know."

"Such as what?" Fenton challenged gruffly.

Eric shrugged. "The story you told me about the night in question... you said you weren't involved, you were away in Kilkenny, all that can be checked out, but it's the background that's so vague. Just how much do you know about the smokies business, Paddy?"

Fenton shook his head. His eyes were lowered. "I told you. It was all just a set-up as far as I was concerned. And the bastard who made the arrangements..."

"You told me you knew nothing about what they intended to do here at Ravenstone. That seems a bit hard for the police to swallow."

"At the time, I had other things on my mind."

"I appreciate that, but if there's anything you do know, but haven't told me, now's the time..."

Paddy Fenton hesitated, seemed to be mulling something over, then raised his head suspiciously. "What's this about, Mr Ward?"

Eric hesitated; he shrugged reluctantly. "I went along to the hearing, where the three men they arrested in your barn, Robson, Milburn and Armstrong, were bound over for trial. After the hearing... someone approached me. The person concerned, he seemed to think that maybe you had information that would be valuable, and disclosing it to the right parties would help you personally."

"In what way?" Fenton asked, puzzled.

"In relation to the charges against you."

"But I haven't been told what the charges are yet!" Fenton contended.

Eric felt they were getting nowhere. "You knew the three men arrested."

"Of course. They're local men. I've met them from time to time at the markets."

"And the one who escaped?"

"That bastard." Fenton's eyes glinted. "I'd know him again. And what to do with him."

"But you know nothing about the organisation he works for?"

Fenton's eyes were blank, but his tone was evasive. "I

don't know what you mean. As far as I knew, he *was* the organisation. It was just a shady business he was running for himself. You telling me there were other people involved?"

Eric was uncertain whether Paddy Fenton was lying or not. "Look, Paddy," he began, "this is all getting serious and I need to know –"

Paddy Fenton lifted his head, cocking it to one side like a predatory blackbird. "What's that?"

Eric frowned. "What do you mean?"

Paddy Fenton rose. "Someone in the yard."

He walked out of the kitchen, into the corridor beyond and opened the front door. Eric caught the sound of voices, a brief discussion. Then Fenton was stumping back into the kitchen. He looked grim. There were two men behind him. One of them, Eric immediately recognised.

"DCI Spate."

"Mr Ward." Charlie Spate grinned at him, stepped past Fenton into the kitchen, looked about him. "Well, I always held the view that you were quick off the mark. But this is something else. Jumping the gun, almost. Or do you *live* up here at Ravenstone, now?" He did not wait for an answer, but gestured to the man standing behind him. "This is Detective Sergeant Chris Jarrad."

Eric had heard the man give evidence at the magistrates court. He nodded to him.

Charlie Spate smiled wolfishly, turned to Jarrad. "And this is Eric Ward, ex-copper turned coat to become solicitor, succour of the underprivileged and representing Mr Fenton here, I understand. And he's here at the farm when we arrive. All very convenient." He grinned maliciously at Eric. "We were hoping to have a preliminary chat with Mr Fenton, but you being here, that puts a sort of more formal ring to the interview, don't it? Unless you were just leaving, Mr Ward."

Eric glanced at Paddy Fenton. The farmer seemed tense, controlling a subdued anger only with difficulty. His fists were clenched at his sides.

"If you're going to interview my client," Eric said slowly, "I think it would be as well if I stayed."

"Ah, well, it's not just a matter of staying," Spate suggested. "No, we didn't really come up here to interview your client at the farm. It would be sort of more convenient if we did it back at Ponteland. And since you're with him, I assume you'll want to be present. And you should also be made aware that there'll be another team arriving up here shortly. With a warrant." Charlie Spate smiled happily, glancing around the kitchen. "And who knows what we might find in this old rathole, hey?"

Early evenings in the Hydraulic Engine tended to be somewhat noisy. The back street pub had developed a clientele that spanned the range of possibilities: groups of students congregated there, from the local college of further education and the two universities; businessmen called in if they felt unable after the stress of the day to face their wives too early in the evening; a scattering of men in the bar from the terrace houses of Benton, unemployed, under-employed or living on the edge of lawlessness, whiled away time leaning against the scarred bar. Two streets away gangs of youngsters roamed looking for cars to set alight, or houses to break into. Eric suspected many of the pub clientele visited the Hydraulic Engine because of the *frisson* they enjoyed, being so close to a recognised centre of criminal activity. Even if they were likely to lose their hub caps, or car radios, or briefcases left carelessly on back seats of cars.

It had been Jackie Parton's idea to meet there.

It was one of Parton's haunts. He was well known all along the river, and in the back streets and terrace houses, the pubs and clubs along the Tyne. He had made his reputation as a young man twenty years ago, a daring, dashing rider both over the sticks and on the flat. He had been a local hero throughout the north, and his popularity had not been dimmed by the beating he had received some years ago from certain interested parties, a beating that had effectively ended his career. It was rumoured the fists and boots had gone in because he had thrown a race; others contended it was because he had *refused* to throw a race. Whichever way it had been, it had only enhanced his popularity and reputation, and resulted in his being welcomed all along the river. No one quite seemed to know how he made a living now, but he survived and he was trusted. He was the recipient of secrets, the trader of information; his knowledge of people and places in the north east was unrivalled, and he had access to the most doubtful of areas.

Over the years he had proved invaluable to Eric Ward. They had first met when Eric was a copper on the beat. When Eric had qualified as a solicitor he had found good reasons to employ Jackie from time to time and what had begun as a professional relationship had developed into a friendship, albeit that of recent years the friendship had been bruised by Jackie's view of Eric's behaviour, and the break-up of his marriage. Jackie Parton had placed Eric Ward on a professional pedestal of sorts, but the pedestal had crumbled when Eric had strayed too close to the ethical line between legality and criminality. Some of the old ground had been regained, but there was still a certain distance between the two men, an uneasiness that remained difficult to dispel.

The elderly Labrador bitch that lay just inside the door, lifting a suspicious eye towards each new entrant to the pub, rose on stiff, creaking legs and managed a slow waving of the tail in recognition as Jackie Parton came in through the main entrance to the bar. He stooped, fondled the dog's ears and glanced around, caught sight of Eric and came across. The Labrador considered following him, then changed its mind and settled back on guard just inside the door.

"That pooch is on its last legs," Jackie Parton remarked as he stood in front of Eric.

"Seems to like you."

"She never did show good sense or discrimination. What are you drinking?"

Eric rose, waving Jackie to a seat. "On me." He walked up to the bar and ordered the usual pint for the ex-jockey and a lager for himself. When he returned to his seat Jackie Parton was surveying the motley crowd packing out the bar, observing with a certain disdain the antics of a group of students, indulging in a drinking contest near the window.

"Getting so you can't have a peaceful guzzle in here any more."

"Rites of passage, Jackie."

"More money than sense, Mr Ward." Parton took a deep draught of beer, and leaned back, stretched out his lean, wiry legs and uttered a sigh of satisfaction. "So, I hear you've got involved with that smokies case. That what you wanted to see me about?"

Eric grunted; the ex-jockey always seemed to be aware

of just what was going on as far as he was concerned. "That's right. Paddy Fenton. He's a tenant farmer on the Morcomb Estates. It was Anne who suggested I might act for him."

Parton's eyes narrowed thoughtfully. He shifted uneasily in his seat. "How is Mrs Ward?"

"Miss Morcomb again, now."

"Aye, well…" Jackie Parton wriggled uncomfortably. "Anyway, I heard about the reivers –"

"Reivers?"

"Why aye, man. Robson, Armstrong, and Milburn, all good border raider family names. Funny that, how the old names still crop up in dodgy circles. Though on the other hand, family members all played for England at soccer, too, so they can't all be bad. Anyway, it was at your Paddy Fenton's farm that the three were arrested. And a copper got his face scorched."

"That's right."

"Bad business…" Jackie Parton frowned thoughtfully. "So what's the latest? How do you think I can help?"

Eric sipped his lager, and looked about him. The noise had increased and even the dog was twitching its ears in disapproval. "The bad business has gone to worse," he commented. "The police have been hanging on for some time now, bringing no specific charges against Paddy Fenton. And…" He hesitated, uncertain how much to tell the ex-jockey about his conversation with Mr Justice Dawson. "Well, let's say there've been moves behind the scenes to spread the enquiry, set it up on a wider basis."

Jackie Parton was silent for a little while, his quick eyes sending skittering glances around the room, missing nothing. "Wider basis, hey? I been hearing things along the river, Mr Ward. This smokies thing, it's not just a one-off up at Ravenstone Farm. There's a lot going on, and not just around here."

Eric nodded. "Ravenstone is just part of a jigsaw that the authorities are beginning to put together."

"But your man Fenton, I hear he was just hiring out his barn."

"That's the story he tells, but the police aren't convinced." Eric hesitated. "They think he's like a number of others on the farms, and in the butchery trade as well. Unwilling to give out information. And now, it's got really serious."

Jackie Parton leaned forward, forearms on the table between them. "How do you mean?"

DCI Charlie Spate, lean, wiry, with professionally suspicious eyes and a mouth like bent iron, had been affability itself during the interview at headquarters in Ponteland. He had removed his jacket and loosened his tie, oozed confidence in his manner, displayed a certain grandiloquence in his gestures, while the cold-eyed DS Jarrad had remained silent beside him. Spate had started by going over Paddy Fenton's statement, pressing him for any further detail he might wish to add. The farmer had added nothing, stressing he had no more information to impart. He had merely met a man called Joe Robson at the market, been introduced to him by other local men he knew. There was nothing he could add, no information he could provide about the organisation behind the illegal slaughtering. But, in spite of Eric's warning hand on his arm, he had made no secret of what he would do if he caught up with the man who had set him up.

"You knew his name, of course," Spate had suggested casually.

"What?" There was a short silence. "He just called himself Terry," Paddy Fenton muttered sullenly.

"No surname? You were happy to take his money, without even asking his surname?"

"The money was good. What did I care what he was called? And he was giving employment to some of the lads."

"Illegal employment."

"I didn't know that."

"But you were mad as hell when you found out. And when you got hauled in for questioning."

"I won't deny that."

"No..." DCI Spate had leaned back in his chair, smiling wolfishly. "But your movements recently, you been chasing about a bit."

"I've been visiting my wife's family in Ireland."

"Yeah, on and off ferries, driving here and there, difficult to pin down your movements really. Thing is," Spate had asked softly, "when did you come across your friend Terry during your travels?"

"I didn't say I did."

"Well, that's interesting, because we *have* come across him. Rolled up in a carpet, and dumped at a waste disposal site. Not too far, as the crow flies, from Ravenstone Farm. Now, you got anything you want to tell us about that?"

Jackie Parton listened to Eric's account of the interview and frowned. "Is that the only name you got? Terry?"

"The man was called Terry Charlton."

"Bloody hell. Another reiver name. Are the polis suggesting your client had something to do with this guy's death?"

Eric heaved a sigh. "Paddy Fenton's been remanded in custody. During the questioning they argued that Paddy's Land Rover had been seen near the site, and that Paddy had been asking around the Newcastle pubs for news about Charlton."

"So he *did* know him, then?"

Eric nodded. "He admitted, finally, that he knew Charlton's surname, and had been looking for him. Beyond that, he's got nothing to say, except that he denies killing the man who conned him."

Jackie Parton wrinkled his brow. "Charlie Spate is going to charge him?"

"It'll be only a matter of time. And it looks as though the charge is going to be murder."

There was a short silence, the ex-jockey nodding his head thoughtfully. "So what do you want me to do, Mr Ward?"

"Find out what you can about this dead man, Terry Charlton. And pick up what you can about this whole business. Paddy Fenton wouldn't be the only enemy Terry Charlton made."

"In that kind of business, if you end your days rolled up in an old carpet with your face smashed in, you can be damned sure of that," Jackie Parton agreed.

6

The sun was hot on the back of Eric's neck as he made his way along the Quayside past Wesley Square to the Law Courts. He had a clutch of files under his arm, which he almost dropped as he hustled his way through the security gate at the entrance, nodding to the female officer on duty. Rather than wait for the lift he hurried up the stairs; he was late for the hearing, but was relieved when he entered the room to find that the court had not yet risen.

He slid into a seat just behind Sharon Owen. She glanced over her shoulder and smiled at him. "I'm glad I'm briefed for the prosecution. You're late, and your own counsel hasn't showed yet."

Eric groaned. It meant he'd have to seek an adjournment, and he guessed it would be unlikely he'd get one. This was the third time things had gone wrong. "My reputation will be shot to hell," he whispered.

Sharon smiled. "What reputation?"

The hearing proved to be as difficult as he had anticipated: the bench was not amused at his failure to move proceedings on. Sharon put the case for decision succinctly. "The accused has been found guilty of two counts of car theft, and has asked for two other offences to be taken into consideration. The prosecution argues that the sentence of consecutive detention orders should stand. Counsel for the defence did not earlier ask for the matter to be dealt with by a social inquiry report. We contend that the court was therefore fully entitled to deal with the matter without such a report by virtue of section 2 of the Criminal Justice Act."

"And counsel for the defence has not put in an appearance this morning." The Recorder fixed Eric with a baleful glare, as though the matter was entirely his fault. "In our view the sentences were fully merited. A non-custodial sentence cannot be justified."

Eric had two more cases scheduled for hearing. He had got off to a bad start, and it did not improve. The barrister he had briefed was young and inexperienced but did finally turn up, bobbing his apology to the court, and riffling through his briefs with flustered fingers. Two council employees who had taken bribes to falsify the weight of materials tipped on a council waste dump were sentenced to twenty-one and eighteen months respectively; the driver of a refrigerator lorry who claimed he was carrying frozen chips rather than two thousand kilos of tobacco was jailed for twelve months; and Sharon got what she wanted when the court gave Eric's third client two years imprisonment for a domestic stabbing.

When the business of the court was over for the morning Eric's counsel hastened away. Eric walked out of the court room just behind Sharon; at the security gate she waited for him with a half smile. As they walked down the steps together into the sunshine she caught the miserable expression on his face. "Coffee?" she suggested.

"Why not?" he agreed, pulling a mournful face.

They walked along the Quayside to the Pitcher and Piano and found a table on the first floor, in front of the long glass window, with a fine view across to the recently opened Baltic Centre, the Victorian flour mill that had been revitalised on the Gateshead Quay as an exhibition centre. Eric ordered the coffee and looked about him: beyond the long windows the elegant curve of the Millennium Bridge glistened in the sun, tilted to allow the sleek grey form of a Norwegian navy frigate slip upriver and berth some fifty yards from the Law Courts building. The frigate's attendant pilot boat waited patiently alongside, dark water boiling under her stern as the Norwegian crew tied up. Sharon watched them for a little while, standing at the table Eric had suggested, then she came back across to him. There were several other small groups of dark-suited people in the lounge, lawyers and businessmen, engaged in low-voiced discussions. She said, "Let's go over to that more private corner there."

"We'll lose the view," Eric protested in surprise.

She smiled. "I've been advised by head of chambers that I shouldn't really be consorting too openly with the other branch of the profession."

Eric relaxing somewhat after the tribulations of the morning, grinned at her. "Is this what he would call consorting?"

She looked at him soberly, and headed for the other table. "I think this is probably as far as he believes it should go." Over her shoulder, she added, "I wondered whether *you* had a view about that."

She was a beautiful woman. She was about thirty years old, intelligent and quick-witted. She was of medium height, and she had frank grey eyes that sometimes held a hint of mockery; her skin was clear, her smile easy and warm. He liked her, but he was uncertain how far their friendship should go. It was too early for such considerations, after his recent divorce. He was still marked by the confusions of his recent life.

"I think," he suggested carefully, "you should have your career prospects in mind, before you even contemplate the nature of friendships."

She smiled, waited while Eric placed a cafetiere and

two cups on the table in front of her. "Career prospects? I seem to end up handling all the mucky cases that come into chambers. The ones that are no-hopers to start with. Though at the moment..." She hesitated, eyed him carefully. "Don't you ever get fed up dealing with the kind of people who come into your office? And the kind I seem to be having to deal with all the time?"

"You were on a winning streak this morning," he argued.

"Hardly intellectually demanding," she contended. "And certainly not high profile."

"Someone has to handle these cases. What's bothering you at the moment?"

She sighed, grimaced, poured out two cups of coffee. "It's not so much the specific cases... a handling and dealing offence, here and there. Those sad people this morning. And more than my fair share of minor drug offences, of course. It's just that I get the impression these young men I prosecute, they've sort of fallen into a dreary existence that's never going to change, essentially. The culture is spreading, they don't seem to want anything else. And I'm on the edge of it."

"Edge of what?" he asked quietly, already guessing at the answer.

She shook her head in frustration. "I don't know how to describe it, exactly. A sort of great wave, that washes around the area. It never settles, it's always seething away –"

"Even though the fish that get washed up are different."

She looked at him with steady, grey eyes that held a hint of sadness. "But it doesn't change, does it? I handle a case for the prosecution, I get a result, the guy gets put away but there's always someone else to take his place. And they're always relatively small fry anyway. The people who are behind it all, they seem to manage to stay in the background. And yet, I get the impression that they never last all that long themselves. They don't face prison terms, maybe, but their existence is nasty, brutish and short."

"Thomas Hobbes."

"I only ever quote from the classics."

"That's a Cambridge education for you." But Eric knew what she meant. Nothing had really changed since his early days on the beat, and yet paradoxically it was constantly changing. Turf wars were regular, kings were brought down, but they were simply replaced by new princes, new deals, new conspiracies. He nodded. "The drug culture is deeply rooted now, like the guns."

"And I hear you've got a client involved in this new trade. Illegal meat."

He glanced at her warily. "Have you picked up anything about it? Background, I mean."

She hesitated. "A certain amount. I've been made an offer. Get involved in something other than the courtroom. And with the kinds of rubbish that have been coming my way in chambers, I've been thinking it over."

"You'd give up the cut and thrust of the bar?" he mocked.

"Cut and thrust?" She laughed throatily. "Slash and burn, more like. And it has occurred to me that a comfortable government job might be more rewarding, as well as give me time to have a social life."

"Is that what you really want?"

She ducked her head indecisively. "I don't know…" Her glance held his for a few moments, then she sighed.

"No, maybe not. Anyway, I turned the proposal down. I suspected it was based on the shape of my legs rather than the merits of my brainpower."

Eric smiled, and in view of his recent experience, hazarded a guess. "Justice Dawson always had an eye for a pretty ankle."

She gave a short, barking laugh. "So you've heard what he's about. I suppose it is an open secret. The thing is, Eric, from what he told me this illegal meat trade is clearly something that's being taken seriously in the north. And there are new people riding this particular wave."

Eric was aware of the fact: it was why he had asked Jackie Parton to look into it.

It had taken a series of visits that took in eight pubs, three nightclubs, a casino, four betting shops, two poolrooms, a floating disco and a remote farm in the Cheviots for Jackie to get some overall idea of what was going on. He found himself finally in a late night drinking den in Wallsend; the clientele was varied, there was some betting going on around a pool table in the next room where occasional shouts of approval drowned out general conversation, and his companion was an old acquaintance, from the days of his pomp, the racing days at Newcastle and Cartmel, Haydock and York.

Joe Podmore liked to be called the Colonel. It was an honorary title bestowed on him by the racing fraternity: he had never held substantive rank in the armed forces, but when he had been in his prime, attending the race meetings throughout the northern circuit he had placed his bets with a military swagger, with his snap brim hat, carefully tied cravat, hacking jacket, twill trousers and polished brown boots. He had been a relatively successful punter in his day but he had not relied on science or mathematics – rather, he knew the jockeys, spent a fair amount on their entertainment, did some surreptitious betting on their behalf and kept a finger on the pulse of the racing world.

His recent lifestyle had frayed along with his jacket cuffs as he headed for his mid sixties; he still affected his customary elegance but the overall impression he now gave was of a measured degeneration into seediness. Where he had once been open-handed, booming in tone and voice and expansive in his bonhomie, he now had a certain apologetic air about him as he shuffled up to a bar, and his tone was less confident; he appreciated double malts being offered him, and alcoholic encouragement of that kind tended to loosen his tongue. But his chatter was never indiscreet, relayed only to those he trusted, and his drifting around the louche circles in which he moved meant he obtained a considerable amount of information, even if it did tend to be unrelated to any central themes.

He accepted a second double malt from Jackie with a condescending air. His pale blue eyes swept a long, slow glance around the room. "Things have changed, I'll tell you that, Jackie. Seems to me standards have slipped, you know what I mean? A rough element has crept in along the river."

Jackie laughed. "There was always a rough element. Part of the old reiving tradition."

The Colonel sighed. "Ah, yes, the reivers. Bold men all. Thieves, rustlers, wild men of the borderlands – but they had a certain style, born of necessity, not like some of the scum who come washing up on the river banks these days. And talking of reivers..." He glanced at Jackie with one interrogative eyebrow raised. "Some of the families in trouble again, I hear?"

"Is that right?" Jackie queried innocently.

"Silly bastards," the Colonel opined. "No sense. I mean, if you're going to get involved in nefarious activities at least do it in a way where the rewards are significant. I do not regard fifty quid a day as significant. But then, I suppose the lads were not exactly high in the criminal fraternity echelons."

"You talking about the three arrested over the smokies business?"

"Idiots. Getting involved with a tearaway like Terry Charlton is stupid."

"You knew him?"

"Well aye. I'm surprised you didn't come across him, Jackie. Man with an ear to the ground like you." The Colonel sipped his malt appreciatively. "Another reiving name, Charlton, but like I said earlier, none of the style. Just a roughneck, a chancer, grabbing at every dirty deal that offered itself to his grasping fingers, no finesse. A thug stupid enough to get into a mucky trade and get caught up in it personally."

"I don't follow."

The Colonel shook his head. "If you start running and dealing, the last thing you should do is start *using*. It was always my view of the more sensible bookies I dealt with. Always place your bets with a man who doesn't bet himself: he's less likely to do a runner when his roof falls in and you stroll back with a winning ticket."

"So how heavy was Charlton's habit?"

The Colonel shrugged, and finished his whisky. He

cocked a questioning eye at his companion, and Jackie glanced back over his shoulder, nodded to the barman for a refill. "The whisper is, Terry Charlton was a pretty heavy user; heavy enough to want him to get into anything, to feed the habit. This smokies thing, now, it's crept up from the south and the tittle-tattle is that it's going to be big business. So Charlton gets involved like a whippet out of the starting gate, but he's stupid enough to not only get himself trapped in a barn, he tries to burn his way out."

"So who was he working for?" Jackie Parton asked casually.

"Ha, well, there you are..." Colonel Joe Podmore smiled his satisfaction as a glass of amber liquid was slid across to him. "New boys on the block, I hear." He sipped his whisky reflectively. "Of course, they'll be relying on cash injections from down south but the network is being set up. There's a group have started buying up some of the clubs, you know. Clubs, booze, fruit machines and cigarette smuggling, prostitution, drugs, and now smokies... There's new muscle coming in along the river. And some of the older stagers, they won't be standing for it. There's a whiff of trouble in the air, Jackie me lad, not the kind of boots and fist trouble we used to see when you were riding still, but real trouble, nasty stuff." He paused, glanced along the bar. "You know that guy over there?"

The man the Colonel nodded towards was leaning on the bar at the other side of the room. He was short, heavy about the shoulders, dressed in a black leather jacket. His face had been somewhat rearranged from time to time in the past, the nose broken, a ridge of scar tissue above one eyebrow, a lopsided jaw. He was laughing with his companions, but the amusement detracted in no manner from the menacing air he wore like a cloak. He was a man who would never walk away from trouble, and would be more likely to seek it out.

"Tommy Berkley," Jackie Parton murmured. "I know him well enough. Muscle for Mad Jack Tenby at one time."

"Before Mad Jack went legitimate." The Colonel wrinkled his nose. "Or claimed to be so, anyway. I'm never so easily convinced, are you, Jackie? Old habits die hard, and once you've got to the top of the heap, it's unlikely you're going to give it all up. Even if it gives you entry to the posh end of the social scene. Mad Jack could buy his way in, anyway. Didn't have to start walking a straight line to do it."

Jackie Parton kept his eyes fixed on the man in the leather jacket. "So what about Tommy Berkley?"

The Colonel sucked at his teeth. Jackie looked at him: there was a certain hesitation in his manner, as he glanced across the room to the man they were discussing. "I hear he's at the front end of the trouble. Blunt instrument. Clearing up the debris from the fallout, so to speak."

"How do you mean?"

"When Mad Jack stepped back a few years ago, there was bound to be an hiatus, old son. People rushed in, like. Opportunities for bright young lads like Terry Charlton. But when you got too many young toreadors in the ring, it gets kind of messy. Disorganised. So someone was bound to step forward, settle things down so to speak. It's been a few years now, and all sorts of niggles going on up and down the river, people trampling on each others toes. Until recently." The older man eyed Jackie with a cynical air. "It isn't just about this smokies thing, you know. Anyone coming into the scene up here will want to diversify, build an empire. And Tommy Berkley, he's part of it."

"In what way?"

"Ha, just an enforcer, of course. He's got more muscle than brains. But he's been cleaning up, sweeping away the debris as I said, hurting a few people. Helping *organise* things."

"For whom?"

The Colonel shrugged. His speech had become a little slurred. Jackie wondered how much he had taken before the succession of malts Jackie had provided. "One doesn't wish to be indiscreet," the Colonel muttered, lowering his voice. "But the talk is that Tommy there is doing the business for a new man in the area. And this guy, he wants a whole, new, clean sweep."

"What's his name?"

"Foreign. Handsome bastard by all accounts." The Colonel scratched a regretful head. "Time was when I could pull them myself, the best looking of the birds. But now…" He clucked his tongue. "Vasagar. Sinhalese, they say. Handsome bastard."

"And Tommy Berkley works for him. What about Terry Charlton?"

Colonel Joe Podmore fingered his upper lip. At one time he had affected a military moustache, in keeping with the image he had projected. He still felt for it on occasions, seemed disappointed to recall that he had shaved it away years ago. "Charlton? Well, it's all a bit vague. One says one thing, others say different. Looks like Terry was working in the smokies business, that's obvious. But something went wrong – and I don't mean the heavy stuff with the blowtorch. No, you see, it's not just the police who've been looking for young Charlton."

"How do you mean?" Jackie asked, signalling again to the barman.

The Colonel turned red-rimmed eyes towards the ex-jockey. "There was a story went the rounds in the old days that you chanced your arm against the big boys, and that's what got you beat up. Is that right, Jackie?"

"All a long time ago," Parton replied grimly. "Too long ago to think about. But is that what Charlton did? Chanced his arm?"

"So they say," the Colonel averred, accepting the drink with a sigh. "Saw a bit of business that he thought he could cash in on. Went for it."

"You're not talking about the smokies?"

"Naw, that was his *employment*, so to speak, old son. He tried something else. Foolish. If you're getting your bread from a boss, you don't start competing against him, undercutting him in other areas."

Jackie Parton considered the matter as he watched Tommy Berkley leaning over the bar, talking urgently with the barman. Then he saw the man in the leather jacket turn his head. Their glances met, and locked. Berkley was the first to look away, but he was turning to the man at his side, making some comment which left Jackie uneasy. It was time to go.

"So Charlton was working for this new man, Vasagar, but got into a bit of trouble with him? Got in the way of the Tommy Berkley clean up operation, hey?" Jackie finished the pint he had been nursing while plying the older man with whisky. "Well, I guess it's all water under the bridge now, with Terry Charlton having ended up on a rubbish tip. Unless it was Tommy Berkley who put him there, of course."

The Colonel placed both hands on the bar and staggered

slightly as he leaned back, surveyed the room with a proprietorial air. This was his stamping ground now that his best racing days were over. He sucked at his teeth again, turned his red-rimmed glance upon his companion. "Water under the bridge, yeah. S'pose it is. But I don't think it was Tommy Berkley who smashed in Terry Charlton's face. He'd been looking for him, sure, just like the coppers were. But I can't see how it was Tommy who put out his lights."

"How can you be sure?" Jackie asked carefully.

"Well, stands to reason. If it was Tommy who did the dirty deed..."

"Go on."

"Stands to reason," the Colonel slurred. "If it really was Tommy, why the hell would he still – as of yesterday – be looking for the little bastard?"

7

The Chief Constable rarely intruded upon procedural matters for two reasons, neither of which was connected with the efficiency of the force: in the first instance he felt he was above that sort of thing – if one had dogs, one did not need to bark oneself; secondly, he believed in principles of delegation which meant that others could be blamed if things went wrong. Moreover, in this instance he had received an approach from a certain civil servant in the Cabinet Office which suggested he would be well advised to keep his head below the parapet, because honours of consequence might be coming his way in the year or so remaining until his retirement.

He felt somewhat confused therefore, when two procedural matters had been brought to his attention by the recently retired Mr Justice Dawson and by his own Assistant Chief Constable who, it seemed, also had direct contacts of his own with the Home Office. That was the trouble with fast track graduate recruitment from the older universities, he thought sourly: there was an old boy network operating outside the circles he himself had massaged so effectively over the years.

But it meant that, in the circumstances, he felt it prudent to be kept at least reasonably well informed of what was going on in his patch. He had already had two long discussions with ACC Jim Charteris since his return from Avignon; there had been a meeting at his club with Justice Dawson; now it was time to hear what DCI Spate and DS Jarrad had to say.

"So," he began, linking his slim fingers thoughtfully,

cracking his knuckles as he observed the two men standing in front of him, "let's get up to date, shall we?"

He fixed his cold glance on the detective sergeant. He did not know Chris Jarrad well. He was a recent recruit from Teesside, whence he had come with good recommendations. The man looked well set-up, chin high, pugnacious lantern jaw, hard eyes. He had toed the line at Teesside for twenty years but had become dissatisfied with his lot, come to the Tyne for a change, would see out his service here. Not really ambitious, they said. The Chief Constable wondered about that. He had doubts about men who denied ambition. And he did not entirely approve of moves to a different force for personal reasons.

"Charges have now been brought against Milburn, Armstrong and Robson, sir. They've been arraigned, the CPS are on board, and we're certain we'll get convictions. Open and shut case. Unfortunately, they're disinclined to tell us very much, so we've not got much further with the wider aspects of the smokies investigation. Indeed, sir, I get the impression that we're not being given a great deal of co-operation in that respect. There's been some dragging of feet. It's my view that we should be talking to some of the other forces, in Norfolk and Birmingham, for instance. Their experience –"

The Chief Constable, mindful of his recent discussions with the retired judge, held up a hand in disagreement. "I don't think you need concern yourself with that matter, Jarrad. Things are in hand. Provided you're certain we have a case against these three men –"

"Watertight, sir."

The Chief Constable sniffed in irritation. He did not enjoy being interrupted. Particularly by a sergeant. It offended his sense of the proprieties. Coldly, he said, "Just see that case through to its conclusions, with what we've got. Make sure of the paperwork. Though there is the matter of the fourth individual of course, the one who escaped after attacking the constable with the blowtorch. I understand he has finally been identified."

"In the morgue," Charlie Spate added morosely.

The Chief Constable's eyes flickered towards the lean figure of the detective chief inspector. He had never been entirely happy about Spate's move north from the Met. The man carried a history. Still, he seemed to get results. "The morgue. Quite so. How far forward are you with that?"

"Hampered as usual by lack of resources, sir."

The Chief Constable was irritated by Spate's sour tone, and by his insistence on continuing to pick at a raw sore. "But you have made progress, nevertheless."

"The man's been identified as Terry Charlton. Small time thug, fingers in the usual criminal activities, worked for others as a minder, convictions for possession, assault, burglary, theft... the usual list."

"So society won't really miss him, then," the Chief Constable suggested dryly. "But have you found any links between his death and the smokies enquiry?"

Charlie Spate shrugged. "We're looking at it, of course, but there's no direct link as far as we can see. I'm still awaiting a final report from pathology, but up to now we still have no leads on the circumstances surroundinmg his death. We've had a team out looking for him after he did a runner from the barn at Ravenstone, but we don't know where he went to ground, and we don't know why he was killed, or why his face was smashed in. *Post mortem.*"

The Chief Constable wrinkled his nose as though he detected the odour of rotten eggs. "You think this might have been a gangland killing, unconnected to the illegal meat trade?"

"Too early to tell, sir. We have a man under investigation: the Ravenstone farmer called Paddy Fenton. We've certainly got him in the frame. He's expressed anger at the way he was dragged in by Charlton so it could be a revenge killing, but things are still too vague at the moment. And matters are dragging on too slowly. The CPS are not being helpful." Charlie Spate eyed the Chief Constable balefully. "And I could do with another experienced officer. DS Start has been assigned to me on recent investigations and –"

The Chief Constable cleared his throat. The sound was peremptory. "DS Start is not available to you."

"But she can be –"

"She has been assigned to other duties."

"What duties?" Charlie demanded with sudden belligerence. "I'm handling a murder enquiry here, sir, and I'd have thought that would take priority over anything else that's going on!"

The Chief Constable leaned back in his chair, his eyes widening slightly. His patience was being stretched: first the judge, then the ACC... and now Spate – who was someone he always felt uneasy with – was getting uppity.

"Decisions on priorities can be safely left on my desk, DCI Spate," he snapped. "I repeat, DS Start is not available." His cold eyes strayed for a few moments towards Chris Jarrad, then flicked back to Charlie Spate, relenting slightly. "You already have a team assigned to you. On the other hand, I hear what you say about the importance of a murder enquiry. This Fenton chap –"

"He hired his barn out to Charlton," DCI Spate muttered sullenly. "When he was arrested along with the three slaughtermen Fenton made it pretty clear what he would like to do to Charlton if he caught up with him. And I understand that no charges were being formulated against him over the smokies just yet –"

Chris Jarrad intervened. "I was told to stand back on that one, sir. I don't quite understand why."

The Chief Constable squirmed in his seat. Mr Justice Dawson and his bloody enquiry. It was confusing people, twisting procedures. He had been warned by Dawson not to make the enquiry public just yet, until the Home Office cleared various recruitment matters. He glared at Charlie Spate, still resentful of the man's tone. "The CPS are still looking at the question of charges against Fenton. But if there's a view Fenton might have been involved in the killing of this man Charlton, well of course you should follow that through."

Charlie Spate muttered something under his breath. The Chief Constable's back stiffened. "What was that?"

"Nothing, sir."

The Chief Constable's eyes narrowed; he controlled his breathing with difficulty. "All right… Since it seems the matter of the murder investigation is suffering for resources, maybe now that we have the three Ravenstone men arraigned… DS Jarrad, once you've cleared your desk, you can assist DCI Spate on his enquiry."

When the men left the room the Chief Constable could have sworn that Charlie Spate muttered again. And he was almost sure the man had said, *Thanks, but no thanks.*

That was the trouble these days, he thought. You just couldn't get the staff.

Charlie Spate stumped his way back to his room, with Chris Jarrad in tow. As they passed through the Incident Room Charlie caught sight of Elaine Start at her desk, hunched over some paperwork; he stopped beside the desk, glared down at her until she raised her eyes to meet his. "Special assignments now, is it?"

She placed her hands on the papers in front of her, almost protectively, like a child hiding her school work. Her glance was cool, but he sensed her discomfort. She glanced past him at Chris Jarrad, began to say something and then thought better of it.

"The way to the top," Charlie sneered. "Cling to the ACC's shirt tails when he lets them flap. That the way it is, sergeant?"

He swept on as she began to rise to her feet, her cheeks flaming. Chris Jarrad followed him along the corridor into his room. "What do you think she's up to?" he queried in a casual tone.

"God knows!" Charlie snarled, grabbing his topcoat from the hook behind the door. "But to hell with her and the old man. Come on. We're getting out of here."

"Where are we off to?"

"First, I need a drink. And then we'll try sleeping with the enemy!"

They found a seat in the lounge bar of the Prince of Wales in North Shields, down near the waterfront. Over the years, the Fish Quay had been changed, Charlie had heard, out of all recognition. He could guess what it would have been like in the old days – grotty pubs, ramshackle cafes, dark alleyways; fish scales, plastic cups and chip papers, and evening pubs disgorging drunken sailors. The Quay itself still sported a few pubs, cafes, fish restaurants but within a hundred yards things had changed. Real property values along the river had shot up in the last decade: money had been poured into redeveloping old sites, buildings torn down, middle-class, electronic gate protected, CCTV monitored blocks of flats erected, and a community of businessmen had moved in, served by the Metro link, sipping their dry martinis on their summer balconies, as they watched the sun setting along the river and the north sea ferries slipping out from the Tyne to the open sea. Not many fishing boats now along the quay, just enough to maintain a shadow of the fishing activity that had been seen in the old days, and to provide picturesque photographs for the windswept tourists.

As a sign of rising standards, the barman wore a plaid waistcoat, pink shirt and patterned bow tie. Still, the beer was up to standard.

"I used to think it's something I'd like to do, eventually," Chris Jarrad offered, "run a pub."

"Drink the profits?"

"Young man's dream."

"When you get older, you get different dreams." Charlie sipped his pint, still smouldering about Elaine Start. "So what do you now see as your objectives in life?"

"Get out of this mucky job to start," Jarrad said wryly. "You put in all the years, you get a pension that'll hardly keep you in fags, and you lose out on the housing boom." A hint of bitterness crept into his tone. "Other people get villas in Spain. What do we get? A resold terrace house on an estate where we once had to put the boot into young villains."

He sounded as though he meant it. Charlie squinted sideways at him. "So your job satisfaction ain't the greatest."

Jarrad shrugged. "Been too long at the coal face to think of change. But I've seen some opportunities go by. Too late now."

Charlie didn't want to guess at the kind of opportunities Jarrad was referring to: a few had been presented to him during his years in the Met. Most he'd turned away from; others he'd accepted, and ended up here in the north only because the powers that be had suspicions but couldn't prove anything.

"So why did you leave Teesside?" Charlie asked curiously.

Jarrad shrugged. "Boredom, as much as anything. Stuck in the same routine. New men coming in who were different from the old coppers I grew up with. Young graduates wet behind the ears; accelerated promotion. You know how it is. A man can work his guts out, do all the dirty jobs in the back alleys and where does it get him? Nowhere, in the end. The guys with the smooth cheeks and unscarred histories come in. Maybe you've made a couple of mistakes on the street and it counts against you. These bastards, they never *been* on the streets so they get a slick path to slide on. So you get to thinking, why bother? Grab your chances. Make a fresh start, even if it is only playing out the years to early retirement."

Both men were silent for a while, reflecting on their own experiences. They clearly shared a certain disillusionment with their lives. "I hear there's been a bit of a problem at your old patch," Charlie muttered.

"Teesside? I don't keep much in touch with them; I

was happy to shake the dust off that place. But what's happened?"

Charlie shrugged diffidently. "Don't know the details, but there's a DI there who's topped himself, apparently."

Chris Jarrad's hands were very still. He frowned, staring at the glass in front of him. "What was his name?"

"Donaldson. You knew him?"

Chris Jarrad was silent for a few moments, then he nodded, expelled his breath slowly. "I knew him. You say he topped himself... Where did you hear about this?"

"Ha, the bloody grapevine, where else?" Charlie shook his head. "Nothing official coming out just yet, either because there was something they need to keep the wraps on, or else they just want to avoid embarrassments."

"Bound to be an enquiry, though," Jarrad suggested quietly.

"Inevitable." Charlie glanced at his companion. "What was he like, this Donaldson guy?"

Jarrad ducked his head reluctantly. "Oh, I don't know, old school, really. Spent all his working life in Middlesbrough. Crawled to his rank the hard way. And at the end, would have had little to show for it."

"Like we were just saying."

"That's about the size of it." Jarrad hesitated, frowning. "But topping himself... are there no other rumours going the rounds?"

Charlie took a sip of his beer. "I did hear Donaldson had been assigned to a drugs bust that went wrong in some way. He was under investigation, so they say. But no one seems to know exactly what the excitement is all about. And why a guy should head for the rope in the attic just because a bust has gone wrong... hell, we'd all be dead meat if we took our cock-ups so personally."

"Makes you wonder, though..." Jarrad murmured reflectively. "Donaldson was all right..." He shook his head as if to clear it of memories, glanced around the bar, then turned to Charlie. "But that was yesterday. So I guess I'm now assigned to you. And what excitements have you got in store for us after this pint?" Jarrad asked.

Charlie grunted. "Just the satisfaction of putting a metaphorical hot poker up the Chief Constable's arse. Going to see a friend of his – well, an acquaintance, anyway. Someone the Chief doesn't like me talking to, because important people in the county don't like it."

"I can hardly wait," Chris Jarrad said and downed his pint.

It was only a ten minute drive along the coast road from the pub to the building in Whitley Bay. The rush of commuters from the city to the coast was well over; the pubs and hotels along the front were relatively quiet, and when they entered the disco it was half empty. A few bored looking girls gyrated in diffident circles around their handbags on the dance floor, there was a small group of young men preening themselves at the bar and the repetitious thudding of the music seemed half-hearted. "It'll warm up later, believe me," Charlie assured his companion.

He headed for the bar, ordered a couple of whiskies, and kept a careful eye on the levels of the optics. The barman caught his glance, twisted his mouth in a grimace and added a little. He knew a copper when he saw one. So did the young trimmers at the bar. They eased themselves away, fading to a table in a dark corner.

"So, what do we do now?"

Charlie leaned back, elbow against the bar, and watched appreciatively as a young woman swung her hips in a long, sensuous motion a few feet away from them. "She'll be on the game, I reckon. Bring 'em in from all over Europe these days. Czechs, Romanians, a few Somalis who've come into Europe illegally. The owner, he'll tell us it's nothing to do with him, he just opens his doors to young people wanting a good time. Claims he wouldn't know a whore if he saw one. Even though he ran them for years, by all accounts."

"The owner?"

"Mad Jack Tenby."

There was no hint of recognition in Chris Jarrad's eyes, but Charlie knew all about Mad Jack Tenby. He could not quite explain, even to himself, why he disliked the man with such intensity. It might have been because of the attitude of the Chief Constable and other senior officers: when a man has reformed, they sniffed, and made his peace with society, he should be left well alone. Or maybe it was because Charlie thought it was all bullshit: panthers like Jack Tenby didn't change their colours or their inclinations. Or sheathe their claws. Once a thug, always a thug. Or perhaps his feelings were sharpened by memories at the Met where he had met more than a few Jack Tenbys who knew how to work the system, achieve a façade of respectability, protest their innocence loudly when you knew they were guilty as hell.

And Mad Jack Tenby certainly had a history, as Charlie explained briefly to Chris Jarrad. All right, he had his legitimate business interests now, a big house in Portugal, a mansion in Darras Hall and entry to some of the exclusive clubs in the county where he rubbed shoulders with hunting folk and landowners with fell shooting rights, but in Charlie's eyes he was still a villain. He was approaching sixty now, but his arms were still sinewy, his hips slim from workouts in his gym, and Charlie guessed he still had fingers in more than a few criminal enterprises in the north. As a young tearaway Mad Jack's favourite weapon had been a pick handle, and he had used it with little discretion. Charitable donations of consequence couldn't wipe out that sort of past, as far as Charlie was concerned.

"We're here to see him?" Jarrad queried. "Any particular reason?"

"Reason?" Charlie grunted. "It's like Everest. I want to talk to him, because he's there." Charlie detached himself from the bar and whisky in hand headed out towards the corridor. Tenby's office lay at the top of the stairs along the corridor, past the discreet baize tables of the casino – and how the hell he'd swung that licence was beyond Charlie's understanding. He led the way along the corridor, but as he reached the foot of the stairs he realised a small group of people were coming down, the man he was looking for leading the way. He stepped back, and waited.

Mad Jack Tenby's craggy features managed a weary smile. He stopped half way down the stairs, took a long look at Charlie Spate and ran a thoughtful finger along one side of his battered nose. "Well, I'm damned! Look what the cat's dragged in! Who else can I expect tonight? If I'd known there'd be such exclusive company, I'd have brought in a few more crates of champagne."

"Hello, Jack. Just a social call." There was no hint of friendliness in Charlie's tone.

"Social? That'll be the day." Tenby moved forward,

reached the foot of the stairs, and turned slightly as two other men stepped past him. One was a typical wall of muscle: dark-suited, white shirt, neat tie but uncomfortable in the gear. Hard eyes, thick fists, shoulders that strained at the cloth of the suit. A deference that fooled no one, least of all Charlie: he knew an enforcer when he saw one and this would be a man who could explode into violence at the twitch of a finger.

Maybe the finger of the man just behind him. He interested Charlie. He was perhaps six feet tall, but seemed taller because of his slim build. He moved with a grace that was almost feline; his dark hair was long, swept back, shining. His skin was dark, his features handsome and clean-cut, his movements confident in their elegance. Charlie thought his eyes were almost black, and his gaze intense. But his smile was charming, a little diffident. Women would go crazy over him. Charlie disliked him on sight. Mad Jack Tenby grinned, almost as though he recognised – and relished – the fact.

"DCI Spate. Let me introduce you to Mr Mark Vasagar. A business acquaintance."

Vasagar stepped forward, extended his hand. Charlie took it reluctantly. The skin was smooth, the grip strong and firm. "And what business would that be?" Charlie asked sourly.

Vasagar's teeth were very white and his smile easy. "This and that; you know how it is, Mr Spate. New to the area. Still looking at opportunities, really, here in the north. And taking advice from well-respected businessmen who have achieved success in their lives."

Charlie pretended to consider the matter carefully. "Opportunities... yeah, I know what you mean – nightclubs, casinos, whores, cigarette smuggling,... I'm not sure you'll find there's much left around here, Mr Vasagar. Jack here, he's been chief buzzard, he's had the best pickings."

Vasagar laughed merrily, but his dark eyes were cool. "I see you have a sense of humour, Mr Spate." His voice was like polished marble, cool, smooth, elegant, unscarred by local accent. "That's very useful, in a policeman." He stepped back, glanced at Jack Tenby and nodded. "But I must be on my way. I am grateful for your time. Perhaps we will talk again."

He moved past the watchful muscle and nodded graciously to Charlie. "And I expect we'll meet again, Mr Spate."

Charlie had little doubt about it.

Tenby accompanied his visitors to the door. On his return he caught sight of the glass in Charlie's hand. "Better stuff upstairs, Mr Spate." He glanced briefly at the silent DS Jarrad. "Come on up."

It was a comfortable room: brocaded settee, easy chairs, heavy curtains, a desk, a drinks cabinet. Against the wall were several monitors: they gave an overview of the premises, the car park, the bar, the casino, by way of CCTV cameras. Tenby glanced at them idly then waved his companions to the easy chairs, turned to the drinks cabinet, poured three glasses of Laphroaig and handed them around, retaining one for himself. He took from them their empty glasses, sniffing at them with a distinct lack of appreciation. "You should know better, Mr Spate. Man of considerable taste like yourself."

"If I had good taste, I wouldn't be here."

Tenby ignored the jibe: he had come to expect it. His

glance was reptilian as it shifted towards Chris Jarrad. "Talking of taste, I liked it better when you brought DS Start with you. Great legs. Startling bosom. Your friend here isn't so pretty."

"DS Jarrad," Charlie explained, irritated at the reference to Elaine Start. Tenby had always made his admiration obvious.

"And this is a social call, you say?" Tenby asked, his eyes still on Jarrad, curious, as though he had already heard the name and was weighing him up.

"Well, that was for the benefit of your friend Vasagar. No, really, whenever I get a sniff of mayhem along the river I naturally think of you. And pay a call. You know, the way a crow will visit a dead rat."

Tenby managed a thin smile. "I don't make an easy meal these days, Mr Spate."

"And you can leave a nasty taste in the mouth, I know."

"I don't need to listen to that kind of comment, Mr Spate. As I've explained often enough to you – indeed, as I'm sure the Chief Constable has explained to you – I'm a legitimate businessman. The past is long since buried."

"But Halloween comes around every year," Charlie interrupted. "So what you got to tell me about Terry Charlton? You know we picked him up off a rubbish dump, of course."

"Charlton. Good local name. I don't recall…"

"Never one of yours, then?"

Tenby walked towards the settee, settled himself into it comfortably and sipped his drink. "Not one of mine. Never was. I still find it necessary to employ people who can deal with… trouble, but that's just protection here at the doors of the club. I keep telling you, Mr Spate, I'm a changed man."

"In a pig's ear. But never mind that." Charlie twisted the glass in his hand, observing the light twinkling in the amber liquid. "I tell you what. We've got too much going on at the moment. A killing. Murmurs of a turf war along the river. Young men muscling in and older men getting shirty. Thought you might know all about it, Jack."

"I'm a long way from the action these days. Like I told you –"

"Who's this Vasagar, then?"

Mad Jack Tenby was silent for a moment, considering options, it seemed. His cold eyes flickered from Charlie to Chris Jarrad, contemplatively. "He's a new man to the north. Sinhalese in origin, I believe, but public school educated. Sedbergh, I understand. Nor like you and me, Mr Spate. The new wave, maybe."

"And what business is he looking at?"

Tenby shrugged. "This and that, like he said. We been talking about possible common interests. Introductions."

"To the smart set?" Charlie sneered. "Or the river slime?"

"You got an offensive mouth, Spate."

Charlie sighed. "Yeah. The Chief Constable tells me it'll be my downfall one day," he admitted mockingly. "But what's the answer?"

Tenby began to say something, then fell silent. Charlie felt he detected a surge of rage in the man, quickly suppressed, and he began to feel he was mishandling this visit in some way. Tenby was staring again at Chris Jarrad, mistrust staining his eyes, and the detective sergeant held his glance, challenge in his own eyes. Tenby took a deep breath, turned back to Charlie, his face relaxing, decisions reached, lines of calculation smoothing out around his mouth. "I hear lots of things, Mr Spate, even though I stay well away from my old haunts. I hear of drug busts on Teesside, and bodies rolled up in carpets at waste dumps. I hear of a copper who's all but blinded by a blowtorch, and I hear of new enterprises in the north. And I hear of new young entrepreneurs along the river too, with new ideas, using old muscle. And maybe I could talk about some of these things, but only to the right people." His thin lips moved into a mocking smile. "Now DS Start, for instance, I wouldn't mind telling her a few things. In the right environment." His eyes flicked back to Chris Jarrad. "But I don't fancy the company you now keep."

Charlie noted how Chris Jarrad's hands tightened on the arm of the easy chair. His legs stiffened, as though he was about to rise. He was maybe too easy to bait. Charlie leaned forward, forestalling him. "I'll pass on the message to Elaine. So is this guy Vasagar an entrepreneur of the kind you're talking about?"

"Time will tell, Mr Spate. I won't. He's been to see me, with a proposition. But I'm not interested." He sipped at his Laphroaig appreciatively and glanced at each of them in turn. "You know how it is. When you've attained a position of respectability, you have to be careful about the company you keep…"

When they drove away from the club, with Jarrad silent at his side, Charlie felt a vague, irritated dissatisfaction.

He had been wrong-footed by Tenby; he had expected and intended to needle the man, prick him into indiscretions, maybe get a closer view of what might be happening in the background to the Charlton killing, find a link perhaps with the smokies enterprise. But he had got nowhere.

Tenby had played with him, even demonstrated an odd contemptuous hostility of the kind Charlie had not seen in the man before. Tenby had not been on the defensive, as he usually was when Charlie niggled at him. It was as though he had been nursing some private information, that gave him a feeling of power and contemptuous confidence. It had been an unsatisfactory meeting; a game Charlie had not won.

He gunned the engine as he waited for the red lights to change. The thought churned unpleasantly in his mind: this had been a game he had simply not won.

At the sound of the engine roar, Colonel Joe Podmore hesitated, leaned against the wall, unsteadily. He was vaguely uneasy. He was unable to put his finger on what precisely bothered him, but there had been a curious air of tension in the Whitley Bay pub he had just left. It was a place he frequented regularly enough, he was well known there and could usually expect an odd offer of a drink or two. But things had been different this evening: conversations he had struck up had been summarily terminated; a *space* seemed to have been created around him at the bar as though in some way he had become untouchable.

The lights at the junction changed. The car waiting there, engine gunning, lurched off with a scream of tyres down the road, its brake lights twinkling as it headed back along towards North Shields and Newcastle. The Colonel put out one hand to steady himself against the wall and blinked, began to walk along the pavement towards the junction.

He was only vaguely aware of the dark car that came gently purring around the corner to edge out into the main road. He was already crossing at the junction when it pulled in at the kerb some forty yards ahead of him. His vision was somewhat blurred, but he made out two men as they emerged, the interior light flicking on briefly to outline them, large, dark-clothed. They crossed the road to his side of the street, and walked casually towards him. He thought nothing of it, still puzzling over the lack of welcome he had experienced in the bar he had just left.

The men made no sound as they approached; his own heels clicked irregularly on the pavement. As they drew near to him, he raised his head. "Evening," he muttered, affable enough in his greeting. He hardly saw the swinging arm, but the blow that took him just above the left eye sent him staggering against the wall, his senses whirling. When he lurched under the second blow he slid down to the gutter. He was half blinded, shock waves of pain surged through his skull and he was helpless, flailing on the ground, rolling as the boots went in, both men kicking him in a steady, remorseless rhythm.

When they had gone, it began to rain. There was a roll of distant thunder way out to sea, a flicker of lightning and then the rain came, drumming on the roof tops, bouncing high from the roadway. Long after the men had gone the Colonel still lay there in the gutter like a bundle of old clothes as the thunderstorm faded, the rain eased to a light drizzle, and the tail lights of cars swishing past glittered red, dancing reflections in the shiny wet tarmac of the road.

8

"They say I'm not allowed to go back to Ireland," Paddy Fenton complained.

"You're remanded on bail," Eric reminded him.

"I had nothing to do with that bugger Charlton's killing," the farmer insisted, glaring at Eric as though challenging him to say otherwise.

"I don't think they've got a strong case. You wouldn't be here in my office if they did. But I get the feeling they have more than they're telling us at the moment. In the same way, I think you've got more to tell. Paddy, I ask you again. Is there anything you're holding back on me? I need to know. If they throw something new at us, I'm going to find it that much more difficult to counter if you've not been straight with me."

Paddy Fenton shifted uncomfortably in his chair. He was uneasy, his eyes avoiding Eric's. Through the closed door Eric could hear Susie Cartwright banging files about on her desk. She often expressed her disapproval of the kind of clients he took. Like his ex-wife, she held the view that he could do better, away from the Quayside. Eric sometimes thought the same, when he met reluctant walls of silence, of the kind Paddy Fenton seemed to be erecting. He shook his head, grunted in exasperation. "Well, if you've nothing to add –"

"I didn't meet Charlton at the market, like I said," Fenton suddenly blurted out.

"How do you mean?"

"Well, I was *introduced* to him at the market," Fenton admitted with marked reluctance, "but we kind of didn't do the deal there. And I did know his name… and I did have some idea of what was going to happen. When he made me the offer, he wanted me to be there but I felt I was better out of it, back in Kilkenny with my wife, giving the sister-in-law support. And I needed the money. The bloody cheques from DEFRA…"

"You'd better give me all the details, Paddy," Eric said quietly, settling back in his chair.

Paddy Fenton wriggled uncomfortably, rubbed one eyebrow with his left hand. "It was Joe Robson who introduced me to Charlton. Said he had a proposal that might interest me. We had a bit of a chat there and then but he was a bit vague, was Charlton, and so I arranged to meet him later. I went along to a pub – the Golden Fleece, it was – and we had a couple of drinks but I was wary, didn't trust him, you know? He told me all he wanted was to hire my barn for slaughtering, and that there was an extra fifty a day if I was prepared to help out with the work but it was clear to me it was all a bit iffy, and I told him I didn't want to know any more. To be sure, at the same time I didn't like him, didn't trust him, so when he left I sort of followed him for a while."

"Where did he go to? Did you follow in a car?"

Fenton shook his head. "He had a place not too far from the Golden Fleece. I watched him go in. I had a feeling I might need to know where to find him, later. And I was right."

"How do you mean?"

"The bugger never paid me, did he?" Fenton's tone was indignant. "He gave me fifty quid and was supposed to cough up the rest when the job was done. Said he had to sell the carcasses first – just paid me that small amount up front. But when the polis came around, I still hadn't been paid. But since I'd followed him that evening, I thought I knew where I could find him."

Eric shook his head in frustration. "Why didn't you tell the police this earlier?"

Paddy Fenton hunched his shoulders in a defiant gesture. "I wanted my money. The bastard had landed me in it, and done a runner, and that left me high and dry. I wanted my money, and there was no way the polis were going to get it for me, now, were they? So I kept quiet, and I went looking for him by myself. Went to his place, the terrace house I seen him enter, but there was no one around. I talked to a few people but learned nothing. The people who live around there, you can't say they're exactly communicative. It was mad as hell I was, and I didn't intend letting him get away with it."

Eric could understand. Paddy Fenton had always been bloody-minded and independent; if he had seen this as his own problem he would have wanted to sort it out personally. "Did you eventually find Charlton?" he asked quietly.

Fenton stared at him, and shook his head violently. "Never got my hands on the bastard. If I had… but I never did, and I never got my money. And then things started spinning out of control…"

"Charlton's body turning up at the dump."

"That's right. I had nothing to do with that. But the polis hauled me in —"

"Why didn't you tell them the truth then?" Eric queried.

"Bit late, wasn't it! Changing my story… and anyway, it would only have made me seem even more involved. And they still hadn't brought a charge of murder. So I just hung on, hoping for the best."

131

Eric eyed him thoughtfully. "Did you receive an approach from anyone else, about co-operation in an enquiry into the whole business?"

Paddy Fenton avoided his glance. He considered the matter for a little while then came to a decision, licked his lips nervously, and nodded. "This guy – I don't know who he was, just introduced himself as Mr Godfrey, said he worked for the government or something – he called at the farm, said if I was prepared to talk to a few people, give them the information they wanted… but I told him there was nothing I had to say, nothing I knew. More than I've just told you now."

"Did you agree to co-operate?"

Paddy Fenton grimaced. "More or less. But since then… look, Mr Ward, I get the feeling I'm coming to the end of a road. The polis have been holding off for some reason, but I'm pretty sure they're going to try to hang this killing on me. And I swear to you I had nothing to do with it. I never laid a hand on Terry Charlton!"

Eric watched him quietly for a little while, then pushed a pad across the table to him. "The address you said you saw Charlton go to, near the Golden Fleece. Write it down. I think we'd better make a few more enquiries."

After Paddy Fenton had left the office, Susie Cartwright came in with the costings that Eric had laboured over. She dumped the files on his desk. "I've gone through these, Mr Ward, and done the time checks that you asked me to do. There's just a few amendments, then you can sign them off and I'll get them away."

He nodded. "I'll get on to them later. I think you have Jackie Parton's mobile phone number."

"I do." She gave him a stern look of disapproval. She was ambivalent about Jackie Parton: she liked the ex-jockey, was amused by him, but was unhappy about Eric's involvement with him. It tended to mean trouble. "You're not going to get too involved with this business about Mr Fenton, are you?"

"He's a client," Eric protested.

"There's talk," she replied primly. "And I've seen this happen before. You represent someone, and then you get involved –"

"You're beginning to mother me."

"Someone has to."

"Jackie Parton's phone number," he reminded her. "I want you to call him –"

"Not necessary," she interrupted tartly. "He's already phoned you. When you were with Mr Fenton. He wants to see you."

"Where?" Eric asked, surprised.

"Here. Six o'clock." She sniffed, turned on her heel. "There's no good going to come of it, that's for sure."

It was an unspecific comment, directed at no particular action of his. But Eric guessed she was probably right, for all that.

Jackie turned up a little early. Susie was getting ready to go home, and Eric heard her talking to someone in the outer office as he finished checking the costings she had given him. He opened the door and Jackie Parton was there, helping Susie into her coat. She was smiling at something the little man had said. "The coffee pot is switched on," she said to Eric. "I'll leave you two to get on with it."

"I wish you'd marry me," Parton said, squeezing her hand. "I need a good woman."

She looked down at him: she was a good head taller than the ex-jockey. She shook her head. "Bad one, more like," she contended in an indulgent tone, wresting her hand free. "And the places you hang out, you'll know where to find a few of those, I've no doubt... I'll see you in the morning, Mr Ward."

The smile on Jackie's face faded as soon as she had gone. The lines around his eyes seemed to deepen as he looked around him uncertainly. "I'll make the coffee, Mr Ward. And if you got something to go with it? I'm in need."

Surprised, Eric turned back into his room, retrieved a bottle of whisky from the drawer of his desk, and got out two glasses. A few minutes later Jackie came in from the small room used as a kitchen, with two mugs of coffee. Eric handed a glass of whisky to him. "Had a rough day?"

"You could say that," Parton muttered. "Things have got nasty."

"How do you mean?"

"The Charlton business. The bastard may be dead, but there's a hell of a lot of trouble kicking around still."

"Tell me about it."

Jackie Parton eased himself into a chair in front of Eric's desk, sipped at his coffee, and took a chaser of whisky. He sighed despondently. "I've talked to a lot of people. At first I heard just general rumours, but then a few names come up, you go talk to them, and gradually a picture emerges. It's not pleasant. In my day, when I was on the racing circuit there were all sorts of villains around and a fair bit of mayhem but it was, well, sort of amateur by comparison, you know? Just boots and fists, a good shellacking here and there. And the big lads, they weren't too greedy. Live and let live. It meant there was a piece of business for most villains who wanted to get involved, big and small. Then in the eighties things changed, and guys like Mad Jack Tenby set up their organisations based on fruit machines, whores... well, you know what went on, Mr Ward. You was on the streets yourself in those days. And even when Mad Jack was ruling the roost, there were always bit players. But things have changed."

"In what way?" Eric asked quietly.

"When one of the big guys steps down, there's always a scramble for his piece of turf. That's inevitable. You've seen it, I've seen it. Then, when a bit of muscle takes over things go quiet again, old scores maybe get sorted, but arrangements are come to between the people involved. No sense in having a war: dog don't bite dog."

He sipped his coffee moodily. Eric eyed him, a little puzzled. Jackie Parton had been around a long time, and knew all about life along the river. But he seemed depressed. And there was something else in his tone, mingled despair and anger. He waited.

"Now, like I said, things have changed. There's a new player moved into the area, with a new piece of business, but he's not satisfied with that new business, he's wanting to draw around him control of all the other activities as well."

"The new business you're talking about: it's the illegal meat trade?"

Jackie Parton nodded. "And lucrative as it is, it's more widespread than I'd imagined. Some of the more isolated hill farms have been approached, and there are farmers up there who are only too keen to get some ready cash, after what they been through these last couple of years. And the tentacles of this particular octopus spread right down through the Midlands, out to the east coast and into the London markets. But it's not just that: the old, traditional business – betting shops, racetrack, whores, and drugs – it's all being drawn in, like building an empire. And people are getting hurt."

Eric leaned back in his chair, toying with his whisky glass, considering. "Terry Charlton was involved in all this?"

"Not centrally. Lower end of the scale. He was employed to set up some of the slaughterhouses. That's how he came to be up there at Ravenstone Farm. But Charlton had a history. Father thumped him about a bit as a kid, disappeared when the youngster was seven. He was on the streets before he was fourteen. He spent a while going in over the roofs until he got a broken leg; after that, his burglaries were more direct, smash operations, the odd Land Rover driven into a plate glass window, that sort of stuff. He was a wild one, not afraid of using muscle, but he also got into the drug scene. Story is he peddled, small time. Then got hooked himself. A steady user."

"Not a good idea."

Jackie Parton nodded agreement. "Anyway, he was still useful, had good contacts, wasn't afraid of using a tyre iron to get out of trouble, or enforce a threat. He got picked up by the new boys. But I was down at the riverside , on the *Tuxedo Princess* last night, talking to some old contacts of mine. They told me about Terry. He was chancing his arm. But what he hadn't realised was that the old ways were done with. His new employers wanted it all.

They were definitely not going to allow entrepreneurs in their own fields."

"Terry Charlton had a sideline?"

"Went back to his sideline. While he was setting up the smokies deals, he started dealing in crack. On his own account. He'd found a source of his own. Big one apparently. Worked with a couple of his mates, users like himself. His employers didn't like it. They decided to make an example of him."

Both men sat silently for a little while, Eric drumming his fingers lightly on the desk top, the ex-jockey cupping his coffee mug in two hands. At last, Eric said, "You talk of Charlton's employers. You have a name?"

Jackie Parton nodded slowly. "The new man on the block is probably not out on his own; more likely he's representing a bigger group down south. But the takeover under him has been real, believe me. He's been using a villain called Tommy Berkley as his enforcer, and they don't come much more aggressive than Berkley."

"And the new man?" Eric persisted.

"He's called Mark Vasagar. Mixed blood, mother from Sri Lanka, father an army captain, the scuttlebutt says. A handsome bastard, I'm told. But cool. And hard. You won't find a personal involvement, of course; he's been busy running around setting up legitimate fronts – a few bookie shops, a night club on the south shore, a trucking business across at Redcar – but the word is out. Not a man to be argued with. And he's been using Berkley to clamp down on the little men. Apparently he has a theory: gnats can grow into blood-sucking vultures."

"Not known for his biological insights, then." Eric offered dryly.

"He's no Darwinian," Parton agreed. "He squashes the gnats before they get too big."

"Terry Charlton was one of the gnats?"

"A disloyal one. Dealing in crack, from within the organisation. By all accounts it was pretty small stuff because he didn't really have a set-up of any size, but Tommy Berkley was instructed to make an example of Charlton."

"Did so, it seems."

Parton made no reply immediately, but he raised his head and stared at Eric with an odd expression in his eyes. Eric waited for a while, but Jackie seemed lost in his own thoughts. At last Eric passed to the ex-jockey the sheet he had torn off the pad in front of him. "I saw Paddy Fenton this afternoon. He followed Charlton to this address. Maybe we ought to go take a look at it, see what we can find. After that, I think I'd better go have a word with DCI Spate." He hesitated. "If I can convince him this is all about a turf war, maybe he'll back off on my client. After that, Jackie, if Spate does back off, so can we."

The ex-jockey made no reply immediately, staring at the address on the sheet in his hand. He finished his coffee, toyed with his empty glass. Eric refilled it for him, and waited. There was something else to come. Eventually, Parton said, "It's a good idea, Mr Ward, that I go take a look at this place. But you stay out of it just at the moment. I got some more people I want to talk to."

"Maybe I should go to Spate now."

Parton shook his head with a sudden vehemence. "No. I want to ask around. You see, Mr Ward, some of my leads came from an old friend of mine, from way back. He was around in the racing days. He's in Newcastle

General Hospital at the moment, in a coma. And it wasn't an accident." He raised his pouched eyes to Eric; there was a glint of viciousness in them. "He got hammered because he gave me some information. Tommy Berkley will have organised it. So you see, as far as I'm concerned, it's got personal."

Eric leaned forward. "Jackie, you'd better go canny on this," he warned. "If these people are so violent, it's better we let Spate handle the problem. I've got a client to clear –"

"And I've got an old friend to revenge," Parton interrupted. "So it's not over just yet. Besides, there's something else."

"What?"

"Something odd." Parton puckered his narrow face, rubbed at his chin with the back of his hand. Then he sat staring again at the address on the sheet Eric had given him. "They found Charlton rolled in a carpet, dumped on a rubbish tip, right?"

"So I understand."

"The funny thing is, that hasn't been the end of it. Seems like it isn't over for Tommy Berkley. Seems like he's still going around asking questions about Charlton. Now I find that strange." His suspicious eyes flickered up at Eric. "Don't you?"

9

Dr Dickson wore a dark suit, white shirt and speckled bow tie. He led Charlie into his office, walked behind his desk and sat down. He leaned back in his comfortable chair and locked his hands behind his neck. He smiled cheerfully at Charlie; there was a certain smugness in his attitude which the DCI found irritating. Charlie sat down, uninvited, across the table from the pathologist. "You're looking pleased with yourself."

"A successful meeting at the university. I've been offered a chair. I deserve it, of course. The money is irrelevant, but I must admit to a certain pleasure in being entitled to be addressed as Professor, in future."

Charlie Spate scowled. Big deal, he thought. "So what've you got for me, then?"

"Don't you ever feel the need to be sociable, DCI Spate?"

"I got a job to do," Charlie grunted sourly.

"Ah, we all have jobs to do and are overworked, and lack the proper resources to be as effective as we would wish and have wives at home who don't understand why we work such long hours... Are you married, Mr Spate?"

"No." An image of Elaine Start floated unbidden into Charlie's mind.

"That might account for it," Dickson suggested thoughtfully.

"For what?"

"Your lack of social graces. Your aggressiveness. Your general air of unfulfillment. As for my own situation, I admit to being a satisfied man, now that the university also has recognised the value of my services and my intellect. And I find the work I do quite fascinating. Now, as far as your own situation, and your professional attitude is concerned –"

"Can we get on with this? The last thing I come here for is a bout of amateur psychiatry."

Dickson stared at the ceiling, rolled his eyes ruefully. "I would have thought that being a policeman you would not have been averse to a certain exposure to the advantages of psychiatry. A useful weapon in your armoury. Need to know how the villains think and all that."

"I need to know what *you* think," Charlie growled impatiently.

"What I think about the job I do? Looking at charred flesh, or fish-eaten limbs; the enlarged liver of an alcoholic or the contents of a stomach; the plump, pale shiny flesh of a young woman who'd been raped and then beaten to death? Blood-tinged froth, damaged tissues, toxicology, distended lungs..." He eyed Spate as he spoke; the policeman's features were expressionless, unmoved. Dickson gave up. He unlocked his hands, leaned forward. "Fascinating stuff. Mmm. All right. What I think about your cadaver. Well, it's all more or less as I hinted earlier. The blows to the head, they didn't kill our subject. They were inflicted after death."

"So what did kill him?"

"Overdose. Self-administered, would be my guess."

There was a short silence. Dickson sat there smugly, fingers linked on the table in front of him, watching the stunned expression on Charlie's face. "*Self-administered,*" the pathologist repeated softly, with a degree of pleasure.

Charlie cleared his throat. "Are you telling me this *wasn't* murder?"

Dickson shrugged diffidently. "You people are always wanting me to theorise, offer speculation to support your own prejudgments, your own prejudices. So, for once that's what I'm doing. Can't be absolutely positive, of course. I can just go on the facts as they present themselves to me, and it's really up to you boys in blue to raise the theories. But a careful forensic study of the subject in question leads me to believe the dead man was perhaps thirty years of age, good muscular development but not terribly fit, a regular drug user, with some signs of a violent history – a damaged knee, old scarring on one shin, an old fracture of the left leg, that sort of thing – but as far as the period immediately prior to his death is concerned, I have been able to discover no recent obvious signs of trauma, which leads me to believe there was no struggle, no signs of violence –"

"His face was smashed in!" Charlie protested.

"*Post mortem,*" Dickson reminded him, wagging an admonitory finger. "The young man died of an overdose. As I've suggested, probably self-administered. Later, the unfortunate cadaver was beaten about the head, rolled up in a carpet, removed from the place of death and delivered to the waste disposal centre."

"You're not making life easy for me, doctor," Charlie warned.

"I don't see that as one of the prime objectives in my life," Dickson advised with equanimity.

"Don't you see where this leaves me?" Charlie demanded, unable to conceal the plaintiveness of his tone.

"A body without a crime?" Dickson suggested unsympathetically.

"Are you absolutely sure about this?"

"Are there any absolutes in life? But, as far as one can be sure, I'm pretty sure that this man –"

"Terry Charlton."

"As you say… This man died without any great assistance from any other party."

"But why the hell would he then get beaten about the face?" Charlie asked, angrily. "It doesn't make sense."

"It must have made sense to the man who felt it necessary to carry out the procedure. Perhaps the deceased owed him money, humiliated him in a card game, welshed on a bet, who can say? Maybe the dead man had seduced his wife and most inconsiderately died of a drug overdose before an appropriate revenge could be exacted." Dickson almost purred in satisfaction. "But scenarios such are these are for you to play around with. My report…" He nodded to the papers on his desk. "My report will give you everything I've been able to find out."

"I doubt it'll take us much further," Charlie ground out.

"Not my problem," Dr Dickson replied, shaking his head vigorously to emphasise that he meant exactly what he said. "My elevation at the university, by the way, will be occurring in a month's time. I shall have to give a public address, of course. It should be something on build up of adipocere in dead tissue, I think." He gave Charlie a slow, oleaginous smile. "I can get you a couple of tickets, if you should wish to attend…"

An hour later, back at the Incident Room, Charlie was able to let off steam with his enquiry team. He observed to the silent group, in no uncertain terms, that it was time they got up off their comfortable butts and did some real work in the streets. There had been no whisper from informants that they were chasing the wrong kind of hare; no information had come in about drug raves that had gone wrong; and where was the general scuttlebutt about Charlton and his habits and haunts, friends and doubtful acquaintances?

"It's just as well no charges have been brought against the farmer," one of the detective constables suggested helpfully.

Charlie eyed him coldly. "No *murder* charges. We're going to get *that* bastard on the slaughtering in any case. But don't walk away with the idea that this enquiry is now closed. Someone was around when Charlton snuffed himself out. Someone took a hammer or whatever to his face. Someone rolled him up in a carpet and dumped him at that waste site. I want to know why. And I want to know who. And you know what I think? I think that bloody farmer is still not off the hook. Maybe he was the guy who rearranged Charlton's face and rolled him in the carpet. Now for God's sake get out there, and get me some answers!"

Reporting to the Chief Constable was a trickier matter. It was not easy to explain that they had been spending time on a wild goose chase. The Chief Constable fixed Charlie with a cold eye. His tone indicated his displeasure. "You're telling me this was not a case of unlawful killing?"

"According to the pathologist, it looks like it wasn't murder, sir," Charlie argued, shifting uneasily from one foot to another. "Unlawful killing, that's as maybe. We don't know the circumstances of the death, we don't know where it happened, we don't know why there was this crazy battering of the body after death."

"There's not much you know at all, is there?" the Chief Constable suggested with an air of disapproval. "So what's the next step?"

Charlie shrugged. "We wind down the enquiry to a certain extent, sir. We have picked up rumours of some kind of turf war breaking out along the river, but the rumours are vague and insubstantial. We've plenty on our hands as it is, without devoting too much manpower and time to the death of a junkie. And it means we can pull people off the hunt for the man who used a blow-torch up at Ravenstone Farm. It now seems he handed himself to us on a plate by overdosing."

"But he was not alone when he died."

"So it would seem." Charlie waited a few moments. "We don't *know* whether the man who took a hammer to Charlton's corpse was actually there when he died, but it's likely. We'll continue with our enquiries, naturally, but at a lower level, lower scale. I mean, there's been an unlawful disposal of a body, of course, but we can no longer treat it as a murder hunt."

The Chief Constable wrinkled his nose in doubt. "Not very satisfactory, is it, Spate? Somehow, I'm left with the uneasy feeling that too many ends have been left untied."

And it was clear that he regarded Charlie as the person who had been fumbling with the laces.

Charlie Spate wandered back into his office, disgruntled. He slumped into his chair, put his feet on his desk, stared at the wall, and wondered what Elaine Start was up to. She simply had not been around for a while: whatever her assignment might be, it was keeping her out of headquarters at Ponteland. He was annoyed by her absence. Annoyed that he had not been told what she was working on, annoyed that he was unable to spend some time with her, to determine whether personal bridges could be rebuilt after the fiasco at Avignon. And he was annoyed by the suspicion that she would be working on something that involved her closely with Assistant Chief Constable Jim Charteris. That smooth bastard got under his skin.

He closed his eyes, concentrating on images of Elaine Start's bosom, and legs.

There was a light tap on the door. Caught in the frustration of his daydreaming he thought for a moment it might be her. He swung his feet from the desk and called out. The door opened. It was not Elaine Start.

"Jarrad. Where the hell have you been?"

"I'm sorry I missed your team conference, guv." He didn't sound really sorry. There was a certain confidence in his tone.

"So where were you?"

"I been checking a few things."

"Such as?"

Chris Jarrad had a blue folder in his hands. He tapped the folder with an uncertain finger. "You, er, you been to the pathology labs?"

"That's right. According to the eminent Dr Dickson, it wasn't murder, it seems. As you'd have heard if you'd been at the team meeting."

"I been with the forensics, guv." Jarrad stepped forward, placed the folder on the desk in front of Spate. "And down in the records room, digging up old files."

"Showing initiative, is it?" Spate asked sarcastically. "They tell me it's the way onwards and upwards, but I don't think it works for men of our age."

Unperturbed, Jarrad nodded towards the folder. "You might like to take a look at the papers in there."

Carelessly, Charlie opened the folder. There were several sheets inside, and some photographs, a few prints. He failed to recognise the face in the mug shots: a young man, wide eyes startled by the flashgun, dark, spiky hair. "What's all this?" he demanded irritably.

Chris Jarrad walked to one side of Charlie, placed his hands on the desk, leaned forward to stare down at the contents of the folder. "These photographs were taken a few years ago. The guy was done for possession of Class A drugs. He was booked in as Nick Hedren."

"And?"

Chris Jarrad took a deep breath. "A guy with a history. Not the usual run of villain. Had a certain talent, it seems, at football. Trials for York City, played in Darlington reserves for a while, as a youngster. They reckon he had promise. He made the first squad, got a transfer to Carlisle at the age of eighteen; he was looked on as a boy wonder who could be headed for Tyneside and the Premier League. There was talk of transfers, real money. But he was injury prone, and he got targeted by some of the hard men in the game. That's when he broke his leg."

"I was never much interested in football," Charlie warned.

"Bad compound fracture. Once he was out of plaster, and recuperating, back at the club with the lads, things were looking up again, though they had doubts among the training staff. But then it all came apart at the seams. He was at leisure too much. Bored. And there was a scandal," Jarrad persisted. "His twenty-second birthday. Night on the tiles with the lads. Fight in a nightclub over some scrubber; coppers turned up to settle things down but he wouldn't be settled. Took a bottle to one of our own. And then, when they got these guys down in the cells they found some white stuff in their jacket pockets."

"Ecstasy?"

"Cocaine."

"Stupid bastard."

Jarrad nodded. "Young Hedren had been dealing. In the club itself. And he was a user himself, of course. The club went bananas, threw him out. No compensation for ending his contract. The broken leg might have finished him, but the drug scene certainly did. In fact it was the end of his footballing career. End of his prospects. And he was only twenty-two years old, with a taste for high living, used to having plenty of cash to throw around, no qualifications, and on the scrap heap. Only one answer to all that."

"Turn to crime," Charlie yawned, his mind straying.

"Beginning of a downward slope. On the skids, petty larceny, picking up here and there, not finding a way back, nowhere to go –"

Charlie was bored. "Where's this all leading?"

Jarrad would not be rushed. "In the file there you'll find a list of Nick Hedren's convictions. Burglary. Couple of cases of assault. Domestic violence – he was living with a thirty year old ex-model before she threw him out after he landed a few on her in a hopped-up rage."

"Solid citizen."

Jarrad nodded. "We've seen a few like him over the years, haven't we? Anyway, he got caught eventually, in possession again. Did eighteen months. Got caught again. Community service order."

"Then back on the streets to do more dealing," Charlie sniffed. "Look, can we –"

"That's his photograph, last time he was booked. And those prints, we pulled them from the national computer records."

Charlie felt vaguely irritable. "Why have you bothered with all this stuff?"

"Like you said, guv. Initiative." Jarrad met his glance steadily, expressionless. Charlie frowned; there was something here that didn't add up for him. He waited.

Jarrad leaned over, flicked open to the next sheet. "Better take a look at *these* prints here, guv. Do a comparison."

Charlie frowned. As he inspected the two sets of fingerprints Jarrad stepped back, dragged a chair forward and sat down, elbows on his knees, waiting. When Charlie remained silent, Jarrad asked, "Did you get a full report from Dr Dickson?"

Charlie nodded thoughtfully. "Yeah. The whole rundown."

"Old injuries?"

Charlie looked up at Jarrad: the man's eyes were glinting strangely now, with a subdued nervous excitement. "The whole rundown. Some injuries, yeah…" He scowled at the detective sergeant. "How did you… what do you know that I don't?"

Jarrad shrugged. "I was just following standard procedures. Doing my job. Maybe the prints give us what we need."

Charlie stared at them. From the records, Jarrad had hauled out left and right hand prints. For comparison, he'd produced one other set of prints. Charlie took a deep breath. "Only one hand."

"We never found the other."

Charlie stared at him. "The body on the waste tip."

"That's right, guv. The body on the waste tip only had one hand, so we could take only one set of prints from him. I ran them through the computer. And we got a match. But it wasn't the one I expected."

Charlie waited, already guessing the answer.

"When I checked the records the name that came up was Nick Hedren. Not Terry Charlton."

Charlie nodded slowly. "Dr Dickson's report mentioned an old leg injury –"

"It'd be the break that put Nick Hedren out of football." Chris Jarrad nodded. "And it begins to fit then, doesn't it? Terry Charlton is on the run after the blowtorch incident. He's a user; so is Hedren. He hides out with Hedren; they take some powder to chill out together, but Hedren *really* chills out, overdosing. And Charlton is left there with the corpse; when he wakes up, comes to his senses, he's panicked. But then he begins to see opportunities, rather than threats. Hedren can be useful to him. First thing, he has to get rid of the cadaver, so decides to roll him up in an old carpet, drive him out to the waste disposal site. And then another thing strikes him. He can't be certain the body won't be found, so he takes a credit card with his own name on it and sticks it in Hedren's shirt pocket. And to further confuse issues, maybe just to buy more time for himself, he takes a hammer and bashes Hedren's features beyond recognition. Who knows, maybe he even *expected* the body to be found fairly quickly. Either way, it takes a bit of the heat from him. We're looking for him because of the Ravenstone Farm incident. When we find the credit card, can't work from the face but identify the corpse as Charlton's, we stop looking for him. Now we have something else to worry about: resources will be diverted to a murder enquiry."

"And we call off the hunt for Terry Charlton."

"That's it. Because he's dead. Or at least, that's what we were supposed to think."

Charlie grimaced thoughtfully, staring at the prints, and the photograph of Nick Hedren. Something else for Dr Dickson to work on now. But another consideration moved turgidly in his mind. "Maybe we weren't the only people looking for Terry Charlton."

There was a short silence. Jarrad was staring at him, his glance keen, frowning under lowered brows. There was a certain tension in his tone, as though he was irritated at the thought he might have missed something of significance. "How do you mean?"

"Charlton's been trying to buy time. He wanted the heat taken off him, probably so he can make arrangements, get out from under, realise what assets he's got. Like maybe a cache of cocaine, crack, heroin, who the hell knows? Something that must be valuable, something that can help him pay his way. So time... and a reduction in pressure was important to him."

"He knew we were after him, for burning one of our colleagues –"

"No, my guess is it's more than that. *We* were out looking for him, but that wouldn't be all the pressure on him is my guess. We were after him but so were other people, maybe."

He held Chris Jarrad's glance for a few moments. "You know what we got here, don't you, Chris?"

Detective Sergeant Jarrad cleared his throat almost nervously. "What?"

"Dead man running." Charlie nodded slowly. "Yeah. Dead man running. *Scared.*"

10

The kiss was gentle, a mere touch, a brushing whisper, a promise.

The blue rolled silently across the green baize, dropped into the pocket with a solid satisfying clunk, but the following pause seemed endless as the white edged smoothly forward, inevitable, unstoppable in its slow, stately progress. It hesitated momentarily over the gulf, poised, uncertain, and then without regret slipped over the edge.

"Foul!"

"*Merde!*"

The Caliph slid a sly glance in Jackie Parton's direction, and shifted his heavy bulk on the narrow bench seat. "That's French," he explained. "An obscenity. Don't want to upset the local clients."

It would take a great deal more than that to upset these locals, Jackie thought to himself. He looked around the room: it was long, narrow, dingy, windows encrusted with dirt, a series of low-slung shaded lights hanging above the baize-covered snooker tables, smoky pools of light into which leaned young, unshaven men with extended cues, beer-gutted has-beens with belts tightened on jeans that sagged in middle age, eighteen year old weightlifters swaggering around in tight sweatshirts advertising their muscle pride, in front of an audience of ex-miners, coughing rheumily after a lifetime in long-gone pits. The constant hum of conversation overlaid the click of the coloured balls as they traversed the tables; an occasional shout of exultation rose with a concomitant swearing, the grudging exchange of banknotes, old men in dirty sweaters and flat caps sprawling on the benches, half-interested in the play, more inclined to nod the evening away, out of the rain in the street outside.

Jackie had been in a hundred pool rooms like this over the years: they were unchanging, a throwback to another time, making no allowances for what had happened in the city and along the river, the end of shipbuilding and coal-mining industries, the rebuilding of pride in architecture and cultural opportunity, the growth in tourism and business. They were time capsules, dark rooms that retained their edgy atmosphere, havens for men who had lost their way or had never even found it, stale cigarette smoke and stale beer, stub-littered wooden floors, a general air of decay, disappointment and disillusion. And they made up part of Jackie's world.

In this particular pool room the Caliph was a fixture. There was nothing remotely Ottoman about him, and if he spoke French it was only the occasional swear word. Joey Califano was of Italian extraction, but everyone called him the Caliph. Jackie well remembered Joey's father: the ice-cream seller had lumbered around the streets, ringing the bell in his pony-drawn, two-wheeled, gaily painted cart carrying twin tubs of vanilla ice-cream. Children had come out with buckets and shovels to follow the cart: the pony droppings were useful for the gardens at the back of the terrace houses.

The Caliph was nothing like his father. The old man had been spare in build with a shock of white hair, taciturn and always in a hurry. Caliph, on the other hand, reminded Jackie of an eighteen stone badly stuffed toy bear: he was bald except for tufts of black hair that sprang wildly upwards above his ears; the cardigan he wore was always unbuttoned, sagging, and he afforded the onlooker glimpses of hairy belly, pale flesh forcing its way through a bursting shirt. He had piggy eyes set in abundant cheeks, red and mottled, and unlike his father he was a successful businessman. Of a sort.

He owned the pool room where they now sat, of course. While Old Man Califano had struggled with his café and ice-cream round, his son, the Caliph, had gone into property – not as a boom-time developer, but as a steady purchaser of run-down terrace houses in insalubrious areas. It was rumoured he owned half of the West End of Newcastle and much of the mean streets along the river reaches, but he never displayed his wealth ostentatiously. He was a notorious betting man; Jackie had known him from the racing days when he'd been slimmer, quicker on his feet – but he was still a man to be wary of, in a deal.

"That lad over there," the Caliph muttered to Jackie, "he'll come to a bad end." The exultant teenager who had sunk a final black, raising his cue in triumph above his head was unaware of the Caliph's strictures. "He's got too much mouth. One day someone'll close it for him."

Seated beside the fat man, Jackie made no reply. The Caliph slipped his gaze away from the young player and rested his rheumy eyes on the man seated beside him. "I heard about Joe Podmore."

"The Colonel. Bad business."

"It was that. But he always was a bit of a chancer. Not too careful about who he spoke to."

Jackie recognised the implied rebuke, and waited. The Caliph sighed wheezily. "Even so, it was out of order. Hammering him like that. Harmless enough old dodger; has to make a living like the rest of us. What's the latest on the old man?"

"Still in a coma at the General."

"He'll need a place when he gets out. Maybe I can do something for him. For old time's sake." The Caliph shifted his bulk, easing his expansive buttocks on the hard wooden bench. "Maybe even the place you asked me about."

Jackie stared straight ahead, his eyes on the nearest game. Casually, he asked, "So you own the property?"

"Have done for years," Califano admitted. "It's nothing much, but it's been a fair enough investment. There's a lot of people want back streets like that, tucked away places where the neighbours ain't too nosy and the polis are leery of sniffin' around. I'd be the first to admit that it's the shadier end of my enterprises –"

"All your bloody enterprises are shady!" Jackie suggested, snorting.

The Caliph showed stained teeth in a grin. "Well, you know what I mean. Some places I like to know what's going on; others, I'm not bothered. The address you gave me, it's a place I don't keep too close an eye on. Doesn't serve, being too nosy around that way. That's where the Colonel went a bit wrong over the years. Poked his nose in too many dirty back streets."

"But thumping him that way wasn't necessary."

The Caliph grunted assent. "It was meant to send a message, of course. But it was over the top. And that's the trouble right now. The new boys, they don't know how Tyneside works; has always worked. They don't believe in giving no warnings. It's boot in first. And that's a bad mistake. Gives the hard men the wrong kind of reputation. Tough, yes. But it loses them friends; makes them enemies." He turned his piggy glance upon Jackie. "We all respect muscle, but we're all making a living. The way it's always been is to put out a few warnings, advise people to mind their own business, stay off a patch. Not wade straight in and put them into a coma, just for chattin' a bit."

"You know who did it?"

"Same as you do. That arsehole Berkley. All muscle, no brain. A local lad too, but obeying orders like they were gospel."

"So what's it all about, then?"

The Caliph was silent for a little while, seemingly concentrating on the table nearest to them. Perhaps he had money on the game. He watched as the yellow went down, and nodded, sighed in satisfaction. "Turf wars, like always. But nastier right now. And I'm going to be a loser."

"How do you mean?"

The Caliph shrugged. "The guys who moved in there, they gave me a few notes up front, but they still owe me money. And I got the feeling I'm not going to see it."

"Who were *they*?"

"Look, I run a business, and I deal with anyone who's got cash to pay what I ask. That house, it came cheap. So when these three wanted to use the place I was amenable. I knew what they were up to, but it's none of my business, and if they want to turn into rockheads, why should I worry?"

"Three of them. Anyone I know?"

The Caliph shrugged indifferently. "It was a tearaway called Terry Charlton approached me. He did the deal. But I made enquiries after he moved in. There was two other characters with him. A no-hoper called Nick Hedren and another waster by the name of Steve Crawley. Him I knew from the time he was a kid, and he was a loser even then. Always thought he could do the score, but never realised he was making an idiot of himself."

"And Hedren?"

"Used to be a bit of a footballer, by all accounts. Gone to the dogs."

"What did they want the house for?"

"A base. Just that. The word was they had some sort of scam going, but I never believed that. The house itself is a dump, even if I say so myself. But they were keen on low profile, and my guess is it had to be crack. But the whole thing was always crazy."

"How do you mean?"

"It's all about territory, man. You can't expect just to walk in and start dealing and not expect consequences. And like I said earlier, the new guys around now, they don't take prisoners. Ask the Colonel."

"This Terry Charlton…"

"Ended up dead, it seems." The Caliph's piggy eyes held a reflective gleam as he stared at Jackie.

"But Berkley is still looking for him, I hear," Jackie said slowly.

"Yeah. Funny that, ain't it?" The Caliph chuckled, the phlegm-ridden sound sound rumbling in his throat. "But it's all nothing to do with me. On the other hand, I didn't like what was done to the old Colonel." He hesitated, eyed Jackie appraisingly. "You want to look over the place, right?"

Jackie Parton nodded grimly.

"Don't know it'll do you much good," the Caliph muttered. "I don't reckon the three of them have been near the place for a couple of weeks. But you're welcome to take a shufti." He fumbled awkwardly in the right hand pocket of his voluminous trousers. "Just the one key.

When you've finished, stick it back through the letter box. I'll get it collected later." He looked round the smoke-filled room as though pondering upon something. "You going there alone?"

Jackie shrugged. "I can look after myself."

"That's what you said years ago, my friend, before you ended up in hospital. So you gan canny, Jackie. This is one time I won't be putting any money on you."

Jackie Parton smiled, took the key and nodded good-bye to the older man. As he was rising, the Caliph put a flabby hand on his arm, detaining him momentarily. "Just one more thing, bonny lad…"

When Jackie left the pool hall he ran across the road and down to the end of the dingy street. A light rain was falling, and the air was cool. He turned up the collar of his leather jacket and splashed his way along to the Golden Fleece. The car was parked in the small yard at the back of the pub. The passenger door sprang open as he approached the vehicle.

"You get it?" Eric Ward asked, as Jackie slid into the seat, wiping a hand over his damp face.

Jackie nodded.

"What did you find out?"

Jackie gave him the gist of what the Caliph had given him. The solicitor listened intently. Jackie was unable to see his face clearly in the darkness of the car. He hadn't wanted Eric Ward along; he had advised the solicitor that it was unwise to expose himself to the people he could be dealing with, but he guessed there was something in Ward that still pulled him back to the old days, when he had walked the beat as a copper, dealt with drunks stumbling out of Saturday night pubs, faced down posturing tearaways, waving knives or bottles to impress their peers, or their girlfriends. Maybe it was the edge that Jackie himself still sought, the keen shiver along the spine when he walked down certain dark streets. Maybe that was what still kept him in the business.

"You know where it is?" he asked.

Eric Ward nodded, and started the car engine, slipped into gear and drove the Celica out of the yard.

They parked a street away from the line of terraced houses they were heading for. It was a mean area, shabby-fronted houses on the hill, narrow, untended, litter-strewn front gardens edged with dilapidated low walls, a few boarded windows, a general air of cat-prowled urban decay. The Caliph had been right when he suggested it was a cheap area. There would be few families living here; the inhabitants would be drifters, junkies, dealers, men who had a reason to keep their heads down, the detritus of society.

"What the hell would they want with this place?" Eric questioned, as they stepped out of the car.

"Just a base, it seems. And probably empty – the Caliph reckons the birds have already flown."

They walked down the hill to the front door, Jackie inserted the key, jiggled it for a few moments until the lock clicked, and the two men stepped inside into the dark, narrow hallway. It smelled of stale tobacco and urine and Jackie's torch beam picked up littered cigarette cartons, damp and decaying, a few crushed beer cans cast aside carelessly on the worn, threadbare carpet. They went through the downstairs rooms; there was no furniture, no signs of recent habitation.

"Let's try upstairs."

The bare floorboards creaked and groaned as they ascended. There was a bathroom immediately at the top of the stairs: cracked chinaware of ancient origin, more litter. The front bedroom was a surprise: an attempt had been made to make it habitable; it had been cleaned, somewhat inefficiently, but there was a table there, a double bed, scruffy blankets. The bedroom at the back, overlooking the overgrown yard, similarly showed signs of recent use: another double bed, a wardrobe, a scarred chest of drawers, empty packets and cigarette ends on the dusty boards.

"So what the hell was going on here?" Eric queried.

Jackie Parton picked up one of the discarded cigarette ends and sniffed at it cautiously. He shrugged. "Nothing big, that's for sure. From what I hear, Charlton was dealing from here, but it looks to me that this place was never anything other than just a cache, a place to hide out, store the goods maybe. It was small time stuff, by comparison with the kind of operations the regular street suppliers have been offering."

Eric was staring at the floor. "No carpet," he noted. "But this area over here, it's not as dusty as the rest of the room. Looks as though there was some floor covering here recently."

Jackie Parton nodded. "I saw that. Makes you wonder, don't it?" He prowled around the room uneasily, shaking his head in doubt. "Mr Ward, I don't think we can take this any further. I was told there was a group of three men used this place, for a while. One of them is now dead; the other two have scarpered. We're not going to find anything here. I've got to get back out onto the streets, talk to other people. But we have to go carefully."

"I've got a client who could be set up," Eric said slowly.

"And I've got a friend in a coma. But we can only go so far, Mr Ward."

Eric nodded, "I hear you. Maybe it's time I went for a chat with Charlie Spate."

"He's not a man I want to be involved with," Jackie Parton muttered.

Eric knew what he meant.

They made their way quietly down the stairs. Jackie flicked off the torch before he opened the front door. They stepped outside, Jackie closed the door behind him and dropped the key through the letterbox as the Caliph had instructed. They set out to climb back up the hill, back towards the corner beyond which they had left the car.

They had almost reached the corner when Eric heard the sound of a car engine behind them, coming slowly up the hill. He turned, looked back; a dark-coloured vehicle was cruising up towards them. It flicked on its headlights suddenly, picking them out, almost blinding them momentarily. Eric raised a hand to shade his eyes. Jackie Parton muttered something under his breath and stopped. Then, before Eric realised what was happening the ex-jockey was sprinting for the corner. In moments he had disappeared, as Eric stood his ground, angry, uncertain.

The car pulled alongside him, and he stood there silently as the driver's window slithered down with a slight moaning sound.

The driver of the car glared at him. "You. Get in the back. *Now!*"

11

They drove away, saying nothing to each other. Eric was puzzled: he was uncertain about the reason for Jackie Parton's flight. It was unlike him: the little man did not lack courage. Perhaps it was because he did not want to be compromised.

DS Elaine Start pulled the car in at the kerb and gestured towards the café across the road. "I could do with a cup of coffee."

Eric got out, waited as she locked the car and then hunching his shoulders against the rain he followed her across to the lighted window of the café. The smell of stale cooking and hovering cigarette smoke hit them as they entered: the clientele were scruffy, the tables were plastic, shiny with grease, the floor littered with cigarette butts and discarded plastic cups. The girl behind the counter wore heavily applied lipstick; her straying blonde hair was piled high and her false-lashed eyes were tired and indifferent. Elaine ordered two coffees and gestured towards one of the tables. Eric walked over and sat down; a few minutes later Elaine Start slipped into the seat opposite him and handed him a plastic cup. The coffee was hot. It was the only thing Eric could say in its favour.

"You bring me to the nicest places," he observed.

Her eyes were hard. "Saving you from yourself," she replied. "Those mean streets where I picked you up are not the kind you should be wandering down. Who was the guy with you?"

Eric shrugged. "An acquaintance."

"Not a friend, certainly. Not legging it the way he did."

"He suddenly remembered he had an urgent appointment."

"I bet." Her eyes were steady on his as she sipped her coffee, allowed a grimace of distaste to touch her features as the flavour reached her.

"So what were you doing in the area?" Eric asked.

"I could ask you the same."

"You know me, sergeant. Not the most expensive practice in town."

"So looking for a town house, were you?" she asked sarcastically. "Now you've moved out from Sedleigh Hall, you need new accommodation?"

It was a cheap jibe, and he gained the impression she regretted the remark as soon as she had made it. He offered no reply. After a moment she shook her head irritably. "All right, so what the hell were you doing down there?"

Eric hesitated. He was not certain how much he should divulge to her. But in his previous dealings with DS Elaine Start he had come to regard her as trustworthy, unlikely to betray confidences; she tended to adopt attitudes rather different from those demonstrated by DCI Charlie Spate, to whom every piece of information was a possible weapon of offence. "You'll be aware I have a client who is suspected of murder."

"Who has been involved in illegal slaughtering," she said calmly. "Paddy Fenton."

He nodded. "I was just making certain... enquiries on his behalf."

"Why down there?"

Eric hesitated, stared at the plastic table top, observing the greasy swirl where a cloth had inadequately cleaned the surface. "I'd been advised," he said at last, "that there might be people there who were involved… who might be able to shed some light…"

"You mean Terry Charlton," she interrupted coolly.

"Among others."

"Name them."

"When you explain to me what you were doing in the area," Eric traded. "Don't tell me this was just a coincidence, you appearing out of the darkness like an avenging angel."

She stared at him for a little while, calculating. At last she nodded. "All right. We've been keeping a watch on the place you visited. We've rented a couple of rooms opposite: I had just left there when I got a call from the night shift to say two men had entered. I came back around in the car and there you were in the headlights."

"You were expecting it to be Terry Charlton?"

She nodded.

"So your surveillance… is it in connection with the blowtorch business at Ravenstone? Or the body on the waste dump?"

"We're pursuing several areas of enquiry," she replied, calmly evasive. "Let's just say for the moment that we knew about that house, and we've been keeping an eye on it for a while."

"Unsuccessfully, it would seem. I've been inside there. The occupants, you might say, are no longer in residence."

"One of them's dead."

"That's right."

"Who were the others? You did say there were others."

Eric thought about it for a while. He had his client's interests to protect, but although Jackie Parton had ferreted out information that was useful, it seemed that the police had actually got there before him. At least, they knew about the house. He couldn't see where a few disclosures might damage Paddy Fenton, if in return he could get some co-operation from Elaine Start. Slowly, he said, "My informant tells me that Terry Charlton was using that house, along with two other men. Their names are Nick Hedren and Steve Crawley."

Elaine Start nodded, her eyes giving nothing away.

"They were all three users, and from what I hear, they had started some sort of scam. Dealing in crack, probably. But when Charlton died... there's some carpet missing from the upstairs room, incidentally. Maybe it was used to wrap up the corpse. You'll need to get forensics along to the house to check that out."

"Yeah, we can do that."

Eric glanced at her, puzzled at her casual attitude. "Anyway, since the death, the other two haven't been seen, it seems. They did a runner."

"And why was that?"

"Because of Charlton's death. And maybe because they were under pressure."

"From whom?" she asked in a tone that was suddenly, oddly sharp.

"There's a turf war going on along the river. People are getting hurt. But you must know all about this. It's why you've been watching the house, isn't it?"

She failed to rise to the bait. "And who's doing the hurting, Mr Ward?"

"I don't know..." Eric hesitated, uncertain how much to divulge. "But there's a rumour... a man called Tommy Berkley. And a man called Mark Vasagar could be involved."

"That's interesting." Her tone was indifferent, belying the comment.

"So who have you been looking for? Berkley? What have you been watching the house for?"

Elaine Start pushed her plastic cup away from her in an irritated gesture. "This stuff is worse than mud… Look, Mr Ward, you've walked into the middle of an investigation that's… ongoing. I don't think that's wise. I appreciate you're trying to do the best for your client, but I don't think this is the sensible way to go about it. These matters, you should leave them to the police."

"I'd been thinking of talking to DCI Spate," Eric said warily.

She was silent for a while; there was a faraway look in her eyes, as though she were contemplating some distant object, or objective. Then her glance flicked back to him, and she nodded. "Yes. I think that would be a good idea. Talk to Charlie Spate. Tell his about Vasagar and Berkley, like you told me. But…"

He waited.

Reluctantly, it seemed, she added, "But when you do, don't mention this little chat we've had. Don't even mention the stake-out we've been running here. And certainly make no mention of my name."

"I thought you worked closely with Mr Spate," Eric said, puzzled.

"Let's just say there's a little problem between us right now." She wrinkled her nose thoughtfully. "He's a bit sensitive at the moment. You know how he is about interfering women. He likes to feel he's in control. So he might get upset if he hears…"

Her dark eyes held his. "Just don't mention my name, all right?"

Eric nodded, shrugged agreement. But he wondered what was going on: maybe Elaine Start was trying to get a jump ahead of the DCI; maybe she was even after Charlie Spate's job.

DCI Charlie Spate stared at the slip of paper on which Eric Ward had written an address. His glance flickered up to the solicitor, sitting across the desk from him in Charlie's office at Ponteland. He felt he knew Ward well enough: there had been a time when he'd had a certain hold over him, but that was a debt that had since been paid. Now, the deep-rooted suspicion that Charlie held towards all lawyers who defended criminals had flooded back to him. And there was the fact that Ward had once been a copper himself: he had crossed a line some years ago, set up a criminal practice, and was to be regarded as one of the enemy. Charlie liked the man well enough, but was still wary.

"So," he said with heavy sarcasm staining his tone, "you brought this address to me as a matter of public duty, I suppose."

"I didn't suggest that," Eric Ward replied calmly. "I'm acting in what I consider to be the best interests of my client."

"And what advantage do you expect to gain for Paddy Fenton from this bit of information?"

"You've been looking for a man called Terry Charlton because he took a blowtorch to one of your colleagues. When Charlton was killed and dumped on the waste tip you hauled in my client as a suspect. Well, I've now handed you an address where it would seem Charlton has been hanging out with two other men. Their names are Nick Hedren and Steve Crawley. I've been into that house. I think that's maybe where Charlton was killed. If you investigate the place, and trace the other two men, my guess is you'll have somebody else to sink your teeth into, apart from my client."

Charlie Spate grinned wolfishly; there was no humour in the grimace. "Problem is, Mr Ward, things aren't quite as you think they are. Things have sort of moved on."

"How do you mean?"

"First of all, the body that was found on the refuse tip, well, it seems that on closer inspection it wasn't a case of murder at all. According to the pathologists, the man died of natural causes. If you can call overdosing a natural way to go." He waited, enjoying the silence.

Eric Ward frowned, thinking. "If the death was from an overdose –"

"That's right. You're getting there."

"If that's the case, you've no reason to proceed further against Paddy Fenton."

Charlie Spate shrugged easily. "That's as may be. But the situation is still a bit complicated. As I said, things have moved on. You see, Mr Ward, the other thing is that the body we found, it wasn't Terry Charlton at all."

"What? I don't understand."

"You say there were two other men using this house, and you named them. One was Nick Hedren." Charlie sucked at his teeth reflectively, eyeing the solicitor. "That's the name we've now stuck on the corpse."

"Hedren?"

"No doubt about it. Fingerprints match. It was Hedren who overdosed. It was Hedren who was rolled in the carpet, and dumped."

He could see Eric Ward mulling over the consequences. Slowly, the solicitor said, "In that case, there's even more reason for you to leave Paddy Fenton alone. There's been no connection between Hedren and my client, and Hedren, you say, died of an overdose…"

"Well, it's not quite that simple, is it, Mr Ward? We don't know who was there when Hedren died; we don't know what's happened since to Terry Charlton, or where he is; your client Paddy Fenton has been heard mouthing off about what he'd do to Charlton if he got his hands on him –"

"But you've no evidence of wrongdoing as far as my client is concerned."

"Wrongdoing? We still got the involvement in the slaughtering up at Ravenstone!"

"Even so…"

Charlie Spate leaned forward and glared at the solicitor. "Let me give you some advice, Ward. Your days of pounding a beat are long gone; I don't know what the hell you think you think you're up to, trying to do our investigating for us; you should stick to that mucky little practice you got down on the Quayside and stop ferreting around in dingy back alleys. That's our job, not yours."

He saw Ward's eyes flare with anger, but Charlie ploughed on.

"Of course, I appreciate you bringing me this piece of information, as a matter of public spiritedness," he said sarcastically. "And I won't pursue the issue by asking you just how you found out about the place. I been told you got contacts from the old days… But I think your sniffing around should stop right here and now. Leave Charlton to us. You need to concentrate on looking after your client's best interests as far as the business up at Ravenstone is concerned. He's in the frame for that. The rest of it, I'm telling you it's nothing to do with you."

"I hear what you say," Ward replied firmly, and stood up. "And I have your assurance that I can tell Paddy Fenton you'll get off his back now?"

Charlie Spate spread his hands wide in mock innocence. "Hey, did I say that? Proceedings against Fenton will carry on in due course, as far as the slaughtering is concerned. As for the rest of it, well, we haven't found that bastard Charlton yet, have we? What's to say he won't turn up in the same condition as Hedren? What we do know is that Terry Charlton is running. Who's he running from? Maybe it's Paddy Fenton. If it is, your best step forward is to warn Fenton off. We would certainly like to see Charlton turn up in one piece. So we can nail him for the blowtorch attack, the smokies, and also to find out what happened when Nick Hedren died. But if we finally track down Charlton and he's no longer in the land of the living... well, we'll have to be looking at your client again, won't we?"

Eric Ward stood stiff-backed, staring down at the policeman. "Charlton isn't running from my client. And you know that. The word is that there are turf wars going on along the river. The smokies business that my client got involved in is part of that war, but it's the only extent of his involvement. You should be looking for a man called Tommy Berkley. It seems he's been working as the front muscle, an enforcer for a man called Mark Vasagar."

"You been busy," Charlie Spate snarled irritably. "Regular fount of information."

"I repeat. It's these characters you should be putting pressure on. Not my client."

"And I repeat. Shove off, Ward. Keep your nose out of places where it doesn't belong. And leave Charlton, and Vasagar, and turf wars to me. You know where the door is. Use it."

Eric Ward smiled coldly and turned to go. "It's always a pleasure to assist the police."

After Ward had gone, Charlie still felt irritated. He rose, prowled around the confines of the room for a little while. He picked up the slip of paper with the address and stared at it. Then he walked to the doorway, bawled down the corridor to the Incident Room. "Jarrad! Get your arse down here *pronto*!"

He slumped back into his chair and waited. A few moments later Chris Jarrad tapped on the door with mock politeness and entered. "You wanted to see me."

Charlie glowered at him, handed him the slip of paper. "It's where Charlton and Hedren were hanging out. With another guy called Crawley."

"Where did you get this?" Jarrad asked, frowning over the address.

"Inside information," Charlie muttered. "No matter where I obtained it, let's just get it followed up. You'll need to send the forensic team out to the house. Get down there with some of the lads and go over the place. It seems maybe there's a piece of missing carpet. Check it out against what we found wrapped around Hedren's body. And talk to the neighbours. Not that they'll tell you anything. My guess is that address will be surrounded by drop-outs, vagrants, and junkies who won't take kindly to helping the authorities."

Jarrad nodded. "I'll get onto it right away."

Charlie stretched his arms, and yawned in frustration. "Where the hell are we going on this, Chris? First we're

172

looking for a lunatic who took a blowtorch to one of our own. Then it was a murder enquiry that turned out not to be a murder. Now it's back looking for a dead man running. And there's talk of turf wars, and drugs and the hell knows what else!"

"Turf wars?" Jarrad asked suspiciously.

Charlie clucked his tongue and was silent for a little while. He shrugged. "You remember that time we walked in on Mad Jack Tenby. I had the feeling he was on the edge of maybe saying something to us, but he held back. And that guy we saw at the bottom of the stairs. The Sinhalese. Mark Vasagar. I'm told he's involved in all this somehow. Him, and the enforcer he had with him. Berkley. Mad Jack, he just said they'd been talking business. But maybe that wasn't quite the way it was. Mad Jack Tenby reckons he's given up his old ways. Maybe this Vasagar guy was just making sure that's the way it is. Or maybe he was smoothing a few paths with the characters who used to rule the river."

"What do you want us to do about it?"

Charlie sighed. "Right now, nothing. Check out the house first. And the lads need to keep looking for that bloody tearaway Charlton. Anything we pick up on Vasagar, or Berkley... well, let's keep an open mind." He shook his head, glanced up at Jarrad. "I see they buried that old acquaintance of yours couple of days ago. The DI down at Teesside. The one who committed suicide."

Jarrad nodded. "Donaldson. We weren't close, really. Worked together for years, but we weren't all that friendly. He was a kind of private man. Kept to himself. I didn't go to the funeral."

"Naw... The past is best left alone, I suppose. In this

business, we can't get too sentimental. But suicide... I wonder what made him top himself like that?"

Jarrad shrugged. "Who's to know? He left no letter, I understand. Loneliness maybe. His wife left him years ago. And I hear there was a problem with something he was working on. Things can get to you..."

"They can that," Charlie replied feelingly.

"Anyway, I'll get on with this, guv," Jarrad said, tapping the paper with the address. "And now we got this name Crawley, I can check with records, see what we've got on him. He'll turn up there somewhere, just like Hedren, that's for sure. Known haunts. Acquaintances. Criminal history. I'll check it all out. And maybe he'll lead us to Charlton." He left the room, closing the door behind him.

Charlie stared at his hands. There were times when he felt uneasy around Chris Jarrad. There was a coldness about the man, a control that kept a distance between them. He seemed unmoved by the suicide of a colleague, a man he had worked with for years. And there was a blankness about him; he was difficult to read, hard to understand. But then, he was aware that most coppers built a protective shellac around themselves, a defensive wall behind which they could hide part of themselves. It was never wise to expose too much of oneself.

And Charlie felt he had exposed too much of himself to Elaine Start. The move on her that night in Avignon had been stupid, crass, and clumsy. The realisation made him angry with himself; paradoxically that anger turned against her. He felt she was avoiding him; he suspected she was smooching up to ACC Charteris; and he was furious that the word *jealousy* kept gnawing at his sensibilities.

But he was unable to get her out of his mind. He recalled the comment Mad Jack Tenby had made to him. He agreed. He far preferred Elaine Start's company to that of Detective Sergeant Chris Jarrad.

Professionally, and personally.

12

Eric was glad to get away from the city and up onto the wide sweep of the fells once more.

It had been almost a week since his interview with DCI Spate, and he still felt irritated when he thought about it. He had tried ringing Paddy Fenton but again there was no reply from the farmhouse. And he could not go chasing up to the fells again immediately: he had other business to deal with. He had attended a conference with Sharon Owen at Victoria Chambers, and briefed her on a deportation case: a Pakistani who had entered the country legally but overstayed his leave to enter, set up a corner shop in Ashington, married a local girl, produced two children and had traded successfully there in the community for eight years. The briefing gave him the opportunity to suggest she might like to join him for dinner later in the week. She had accepted with a smile.

He had taken a call from Anne, who had asked him what was happening with the Paddy Fenton issue: from her guarded remarks he guessed she had more than an inkling about the arrangements being set up by Mr Justice Dawson, and he was not surprised. His ex-wife moved in all the right circles of power: information leaks would be common among the Northumberland gentry and their social associates. She felt that Paddy should be encouraged to co-operate with Dawson's people.

The rest of the week seemed to be frittered away with meetings with clients, most of them surprisingly inconclusive: a Croatian man charged with a fraudulent marriage, a small businessman faced with charges of passing forged bank notes; a persistent offender in an indecent assault case and two layabouts conspiring to manufacture amphetamines; possession of an offensive weapon, a breach of parole licence, domestic violence involving a large wife and a timid husband, stolen microchips, pornographic photographs, credit card fraud… It was a week when Eric thought that maybe his secretary Susie Cartwright was right. She was only echoing what others had said often enough. There had to be better things to do with his life.

And Jackie Parton had not been in touch since he had fled upon Elaine Start's approach.

Not until Friday morning did he call.

"Mr Ward?"

"Jackie! You've been making yourself scarce."

There was a short silence during which Eric could hear the ex-jockey's even breathing. "Look, I'm sorry about the other evening. I thought it was best to get the hell out of there. I guessed it would be the polis. If it wasn't, if it was the other lot, it would have been me they was after anyway, not you."

"The other lot being…?"

"Tommy Berkley. But I don't think it's on really. He's already made his point, the bastard, with his bashing of the Colonel."

"How did you know it might have been the police, anyway?"

Jackie Parton was silent for a moment. "I didn't give you the full story earlier. When I was about to leave the pool room, my contact, he told me that the coppers was keeping the address under surveillance. There's no chance of his not knowing about something like that, not in that area. He didn't know why they was watching, but it was probably why the two villains had scarpered. He's pretty sure that's where the accident occurred."

"Accident? You mean Nick Hedren overdosing?"

"You heard about that, then." Jackie cleared his throat nervously. "Yeah, it was Hedren, I understand, and Terry Charlton is still on the run."

"Berkley is still looking for him?"

"Like always. The story is they want to make an example of him: discourage anyone else from muscling in on the turf. And I think they want to know where he got his supply from too. There's something funny about that, by the way…"

"Jackie, I've been warned off. Told this is all police business and we should keep out of it. I think it's good advice. Let other people slug it out."

There was a short silence. "I'm not surprised the polis would say that," Jackie replied at last. "But the Colonel is still in a coma. So we'll have to see about that. Anyway, I was just ringing to let you know the way things were – and to tell you about Hedren, if you didn't know already. Was it the polis told you?"

"DCI Spate."

"Right… Did he have anything to say about the source of the crack Charlton's been dealing?"

"It wasn't discussed."

"Okay… Well, I'll stay in touch, Mr Ward."

The call jogged Eric; he still hadn't spoken with Paddy Fenton. He decided he had better go back up to Ravenstone, to talk to the farmer, to bring him up to date with recent developments. Not least the fact that Terry Charlton was still alive.

* * *

The bracken had lost its golden russet colour on the lower slopes of the fell and now spread up to the ridges in a dull green carpet. Eric had walked these ridges often, towards the bare Cheviot summit plateau where ravens called and falcons hovered almost motionless, scanning the scree bilberry and harebell, wood sage and woodrush, searching the undergrowth for signs of movement, the scurrying of rabbits or mice or voles seeking safety from the predatory talons. He caught brief glimpses of shy feral goats, grey-blue in colour, feeding among the rough grazing of the moorland, deer sedge and cotton grass, but he left them behind him as he crossed the ridge on the long looping road, and dropped down past the purple moor grass and heather to reach the bridge at the valley bottom and climb again towards the enclosed farmland acreage of Ravenstone.

As he entered the track towards the farm itself he could see that someone was certainly at home: a thin trail of grey smoke ascended in the still air, a dark stain against the sharp blue of the afternoon sky.

He parked directly in front of the house. Chickens scattered at his approach: they seemed somehow plumper and happier than when he had last seen them, but it could have been his imagination. The yard also was tidier, recently weeded; the flower borders cleaned in the last few days, it seemed.

He heard some barking and Paddy Fenton's border collie came bounding around from the side of the house, suspicious and growling but recognising Eric, the dog fussed around his feet as he put down a hand to stroke its ears. The dog followed him along the path; he knocked on the door to the farmhouse and there was a short delay. When the door opened, he realised that Margaret Fenton had returned home.

"Mr Ward! This is unexpected."

She had lost weight since he had last seen her. Margaret Fenton was not a tall woman; she had always been slim, almost fragile in build, and her pale, blue-veined skin seemed to emphasise the smallness of her frame. Her hair was auburn, but now he detected streaks of grey, and there were lines of anxiety around her mouth. Her eyes were deep-shadowed, and clearly the recent months, staying with her sister in Kilkenny, had been a considerable strain for her.

As she stepped back, inviting him in, she led the way to the parlour at the front of the house rather than the kitchen at the back. The room was cold and formal: a mantelpiece lined with faded photographs of people in Edwardian poses; patterned carpet, heavy wallpaper, a settee and two easy chairs, shiny imitation leather all stiffly presented, rarely used, the reception room for well-regarded visitors. It was a practice that was dated, old-worldly, and Eric sat on the edge of the chair, feeling ill at ease. He declined the offer of a cup of tea.

"I'm sorry to hear about your sister, Margaret."

"Aye, well, it's all over now. Eighteen months it took, and it was sad to see her fade away. She had been a bonny woman, in her prime. And the pain… you could see it in her eyes, Mr Ward, that was the terrible thing. In the end, it was a merciful release."

"You stayed with her."

"To the end, yes." She touched the heel of her hand to one eye, prickling with tears. "And Paddy was good. He came over to Kilkenny as often as he could. But there's still the stock to care for, and with the troubles back here..." Her wounded eyes flitted glances around the corners of the room as though seeking solutions that stubbornly avoided her. "What's been going on, Mr Ward? I'm worried about Paddy. He's tried to keep things away from me in my family troubles, and I can understand that, but all this business with the police is something else again, and he seems to be going out all the time I don't know where. He won't tell me. He's just not *talking* to me, you know, the way he always used to? I don't know what's happening, and I feel that somehow I'm letting him down, not being here for him in his own troubles."

"I'm sure it'll all turn out well enough, Margaret," Eric soothed.

"It was what Mrs Ward said, when she called to pay her respects." Margaret Fenton hesitated, remembering that Eric and Anne had parted. "She's been very good."

Eric nodded. "We all know what you've been going through. As for Paddy... well, I imagine you know how foolish he's been. He'll have told you all about the business here at the barn."

She nodded, her eyes glistening. "I know all about that, and I gave him a piece of my mind about it when he told me at home in Kilkenny. If I'd been here at the farm it just wouldn't have happened. But it was a bad time, and I was away... maybe I spoke too harshly when he had the troubles on his own shoulders. But he's said nothing much since, and he's kind of withdrawn, you know, Mr Ward?"

"He's a stubborn, proud man, Margaret."

"Aye, I know that well enough. But I can't help being worried. Of recent days he's taken to going out on the

182

fell. He says he's up with the stock, what few we have left, but I know it's otherwise. To start with, he's not been taking the dog with him. He's been visiting the other hill farms, I know, because there's been a few calls from farming neighbours. He's taken them out of my hearing. I think it's because he doesn't want to worry me, but it's worried I am. He's changed, he's harder, I don't seem to be able to communicate with him."

"Is that where he is at the moment? On the fell?"

She turned her eyes upon him and stared at him, indecision marking her mouth. "I think so. You got to realise, Mr Ward, I've been worried. It's not something I would normally do. But he's just stopped talking to me, and I can't get close to him. I'm at my wit's end. It's not like me to get suspicious, try to check on him –"

"What's happened?"

"These phone calls… he takes them upstairs, away from me in the kitchen, on the extension. And then he goes out. But this afternoon I was at the end of my tether. We'd had a few words, and there was a coolness between us. Then the phone rang, and he went upstairs to take it, like he knew who it was who'd be ringing, and he didn't want me to hear. It's not something I would normally do, but I was angry…"

"You listened in?"

"Just for a moment. It wasn't a long call. I picked up the extension, just as the call was ending."

"Who was Paddy speaking to?"

She shook her head, touched her hair with a nervous, uncertain hand. "It wasn't a voice I recognised. And it was sort of muffled. And then Paddy put the phone down, and he came back downstairs and he went out, without a word. He sent the dog back when she tried to climb in with him, and he went off by himself in the Land Rover. I'm worried, Mr Ward. I don't know what he's getting himself into. And he won't talk to me!"

"Did you hear anything on the phone, that might –"

"I just caught one thing. There was mention of Auchope Farm. I think that's where Paddy's headed. But I don't know why! What's going on, Mr Ward? He's so strange, so grim, so unlike himself. You know he can be headstrong, and stubborn, but those moods are short-lived, when he flares up. This is different. He seems *committed* to something."

"Auchope Farm." Eric was silent for a little while. "That'll be up Harthope Valley way, I seem to recall."

She nodded. There was a hint of fear in her eyes. "You'll go up there, Mr Ward? Paddy's not long gone – maybe an hour since."

Eric reached out, patted her hand reassuringly. "I'll go up there, Margaret. I'll try to find out what's going on."

Eric knew the valley. It was a beautiful, lonely place, long ago formed by a geological fault, smoothed by the action of glaciers. A singe track road led to the heart of the valley, winding down to Skirl Naked past Carey Burn and Hawsen Burn, and rising to some scattered, isolated farms on the fell. Regular flooding over the years caused by Harthope Burn had meant that the fields on the floor of Harthope Valley had been unenclosed and unimproved: the braided course of the burn had left grassy spaces, gorse-strewn terraces and areas of willow scrub on the wet, undrained land where sheep had formerly grazed. None grazed there now. The scars left by the devastation of the foot and mouth outbreak had led to the older, disillusioned farmers giving up their tenancies, and there were no younger men ready and willing to replace them. Several of the farms were now empty, disused, grass already growing in cobbled yards, and the land was turning back to ungrazed wild scrub, gorse, bracken, sedge and bog mosses.

Auchope Farm was on a wild, isolated hill. It had never been one of the better holdings, Eric recalled. He had ridden up here from Sedleigh Hall years ago, and it had been a struggling property then. He had heard it had been abandoned by the last tenant, a sixty-year-old Northumbrian, some two years ago. The property was as he remembered it: a dark, stone-roofed longhouse, living accommodation and barn attached, with a cobbled yard at the back, scrawny sycamore trees crouching windblown to one side, a meagre protection for the house from the winter gales that buffeted down from the fell. Eric expected the scene of isolation as he drove over the hill overlooking Auchope, but as he looked across the narrow burn, and headed for the bridge, he realised there was activity at the deserted farm.

From the hill crest he could make out a dark blue Land Rover parked in the yard in front of the house; he suspected it might be Paddy Fenton's. Drawn up alongside it, slanted across its nose as though to prevent its removal was another vehicle, a four door saloon car. And crossing the bridge at the foot of the hill below Eric was yet another vehicle, a yellow and black police car, blue light flashing on the roof. As he dropped down the winding track towards the bridge, he saw the police car come to a halt in the yard. There was a man standing in the doorway of the farmhouse, gesticulating towards the fell. A policeman in yellow jacket stepped out of the car, joined his companion, and they disappeared, running around the back of the house.

Eric crossed the bridge, drove up the lumpy track to Auchope Farm. He got out of the car. The air seemed cold, and the yard was in gloomy shadow. He walked to the back of the house, puzzled. On the fell rising behind the house he caught sight of the yellow-jacketed police officer scrambling through the heather, the other, plain-clothed man in front of him, heading for the ridge and the scar beyond.

Eric went back to the front of the farmhouse. He looked at the Land Rover, put his hand on the bonnet. The metal was still warm. Paddy could not have been at the farm for very long. He hesitated, then walked through the open door of the farmhouse. The corridor was dark, a damp chill to the air. He made his way forward into the kitchen. He met a scene of disorder. The heavy table had been overturned, the floor was littered, some crockery smashed in the hearth. The back door, leading to the yard and the fell beyond, was open.

Eric turned, and it was then that he saw the man lying behind the kitchen door. He stopped, a cold surge spreading through his veins. He noted the jeans, the windcheater, the fair hair, thick and matted, the sightless eyes, wide and staring. A heavy, dark stain had come from the man's head, coagulating on the cold stone of the flagged floor. The face was scarred with a gaping wound. The man was dead.

Eric took a deep breath. Paddy Fenton's Land Rover was in the yard. Two policemen were scrambling on the fell. Margaret Fenton had indeed had cause to worry. If the death of Nick Hedren had probably been accidental, this was certainly not.

This was murder.

13

Chris Jarrad was the first to re-enter the sparsely furnished interview room where Eric sat with Paddy Fenton. He nodded to Eric, gave the farmer a long, hard stare and sat down beside the tape recorder. Nothing was said. A few minutes later DCI Charlie Spate came in and took the chair opposite Eric. He folded his arms, and nodded slowly. "Well, so here we are again. This is getting to be like home from home for you, hey, Mr Fenton?"

Eric glanced at his client, who remained silent, glowering at Spate. Eric hesitated. "Mr Fenton is happy to answer any questions you might wish to put to him. I have advised him that he need say nothing, but he wishes to co-operate fully in this enquiry."

"I bet he does," Spate replied, smiling, casting a cynical glance sideways at Chris Jarrad. "Now we got the bugger bang to rights."

"What's that supposed to mean?" Eric asked, as Paddy Fenton shuffled sullenly in his seat beside him.

"It means we got a dead man at a deserted farmhouse, and another man who leaves his car there at the scene and tries to do a runner over the fell when the police arrive. What's the Latin for that?"

"*Quod erat demonstrandum*," Jarrad said obligingly. "QED."

There was a short silence. As the tension grew in the narrow little room Paddy Fenton cleared his throat, seemed to be about to speak until Eric placed a restraining hand on his arm. "Yes," he murmured. "The police arrived. In two cars. Just how did that come about, Mr Spate? At that particular time."

Spate leaned back comfortably, confident. "Chris, you can tell our friend here how it happened."

Chris Jarrad's tone was wooden, flat, almost as though he were repeating a meaningless catechism. "Since the realisation that the body found on the waste tip was that of Nick Hedren, rather than the person we thought it was – Terry Charlton – we've stepped up our search for Charlton and his companion. Steve Crawley." His cold eyes flickered over Eric. "The address you gave us, it was where the three of them seemed to have hung out together, dealing in crack."

"We've found traces," Charlie Spate interrupted, "our forensic boys have gone over the place with a fine toothcomb, as they say. Oh, and the strip of carpet used to roll up Hedren's body, that came from the house, as you thought it might have done. You've been a big help, Mr Ward. To us at least."

Paddy Fenton glanced quickly at Eric, but said nothing with Eric's hand still on his arm.

"A check of the police records," Chris Jarrad continued, "soon threw up information about Steve Crawley. A local lad – not to Newcastle, but to Northumberland. He was brought up on a farm, by his uncle. Illegitimate, not very bright, and not all that happy with a farm labourer's life, he left the county when his uncle died and came along to Tyneside. Wasn't long before he started running with the wrong people, picking up enough to live on by burglary, car theft. Several convictions, a short time inside, but nothing much heard of him for the last two years. His history meant we decided we ought to extend our search to the county, rather than merely follow up leads on Tyneside. Mr Spate asked me to head up a team, and that's what we were doing. My colleague and I were in separate cars, working the more remote farms; he was just across the valley when I arrived at Auchope. I saw the Land Rover, and looked around. No sign of anyone."

"Because your client had already gone out at the back door, and was legging it up the fell," Spate interrupted amiably. "Soon as he saw the police car."

"I entered the building; the door was open," Jarrad continued. "Inside, I found the body in the kitchen. I radioed for backup, my colleague arrived in his car from across the valley, and it's then we realised the owner of the Land Rover was on the fell."

"Bad mistake," Spate added, shaking his head at Paddy Fenton. "I mean, all that expense you caused us, bringing up a helicopter, chasing you all day across that moorland. For what, if you were innocent?"

"I panicked," Fenton said angrily, pushing aside Eric's restraining hand. "I went in the house, saw the body like you did, and then heard the first car coming. I didn't know it was a police car, wasn't thinking straight, didn't know what to do. I just panicked, hid out the back until I could think, then the second car came – the blue light was flashing – and that's when I took to the fell."

"So if the second car hadn't arrived, you'd have tried to do to the detective sergeant here what you did to the guy inside the farmhouse?" Spate asked.

"I didn't do anything in there! The man was already dead when I arrived."

"Oh, we don't doubt it," Spate agreed easily.

There was a short silence. Eric watched Charlie Spate carefully. He frowned, not understanding. "If you agree the man was dead before my client arrived, why on earth –"

DCI Spate held up a warning hand. "Oh, no, wait a minute. Let's be clear what I'm saying. Your client arrived there minutes before DS Jarrad did, but that wouldn't have been his *first* visit, would it? He'd come back, to sort out what he was going to do with the body. What, bury it, Paddy? Chuck it in the tarn just three miles away? What was your intention?"

"I don't know what you're talking about! I didn't even know who the man was!"

Charlie Spate smiled indulgently. "Ah, well, maybe we'll take that with a pinch of salt. Maybe we'll just disbelieve you. My guess is he wasn't the man you were looking for. You were really still trying to find our elusive Mr Charlton, weren't you?"

Paddy Fenton began to speak, but Eric interrupted quickly. "What makes you believe my client was looking for Charlton?"

Charlie Spate sneered impatiently. "Aw, come on Mr Ward! We got a bit of history here! First of all, your client was involved with Terry Charlton over the smokies business up at Ravenstone. And secondly, we have it on record that he's been running around saying what he'll do to Charlton's face when he finds him."

"The dead man at Auchope was not Terry Charlton," Eric interrupted in an even tone. "I understand the corpse has been identified as that of Steve Crawley."

"That's so," Spate replied with a certain enthusiasm. "The second of the three musketeers. But Mr Fenton here knew Steve Crawley –"

"That's not so. I never met him –"

"Or even if he didn't actually know him, he knew of him, knew he was a mucker of Terry Charlton, and when he arrived at the farm and met Crawley hiding out there, he decided to beat the hell out of him to find out where Charlton had disappeared to!"

"You've no evidence of that," Eric said coldly.

"Evidence? Maybe we'll yet find some prints, some DNA, some blood spattering on your client's clothing. It's early days yet. But there's enough by way of connections to allow us to start building a story here. Not least because we caught your client there at the farm, with the corpse, and when we arrive, he's legging it. Innocent men don't need to run, you should know that, Ward!"

Eric was silent for a few moments. He had had a long argument with Paddy Fenton, advising him that there was no need for him to say anything at this stage, but the Irishman was adamant. He was angry, disturbed, and anxious about what his wife Margaret might be thinking. He wanted to set the record straight as far as he was concerned. Reluctantly, Eric said, "Against my advice, Mr Fenton would like to make a statement at this time."

Charlie Spate smiled wolfishly. "Well, he's been read his rights, so he knows the score. I'm pleased that he feels he wishes to co-operate with us. Mr Jarrad here will switch on the tape, so we have a record of the statement. Then we'll take things from there."

There was a short silence. Jarred switched on the tape recorder, murmured the details of the interview and then sat back, his lantern jaw stiff-set, his eyes fixed on Paddy Fenton.

The Irishman took a deep, shuddering breath. "This is the way it was. I got involved with Terry Charlton when he offered me three hundred quid a day for the use of my barn for slaughtering. I knew that he was employing Milburn, and Armstrong and Robson, but I never met anybody else he was involved with. Like this man Crawley."

He hesitated, licked his dry lips. Spate nodded. "Go on."

"I thought over the offer Charlton made to me at the market, then I met him again later, took the deposit he offered me. After that I joined my wife at her sister's in Kilkenny. A few days later I was called back to England, from Kilkenny, after the police raid at Ravenstone. And, I admit, I was mad as hell at Charlton because of the mess he had landed me in. And I went looking for him –"

"Paddy…" Eric warned.

"No, Mr Ward, let's get it all out in the open," the farmer insisted angrily. "I went looking for that bastard because he hadn't paid me all he owed me, and he'd got me into trouble and the police were threatening to indict me for his murder –"

"But it wasn't murder," Eric interrupted for the record, "it wasn't murder and it wasn't Charlton, it was Nick Hedren overdosing himself."

Spate shrugged non-committally. "Makes no difference what was happening then, what's important is what happened since. We've been looking for Charlton, but so has your client."

"Yes, I was still looking for him, but things were different," Fenton blurted out desperately. He cast a quick glance at Eric. "The fact is, I was still mad as hell at him, and still worried while I thought you were going to prosecute me for murder as well as hiring out my barn for illegal activities, but then I got an approach."

"An approach?" Spate asked quietly. "What kind of approach?"

Paddy Fenton hesitated. "There was this guy… he was from the Home Office, he said. Introduced himself as a Mr Godfrey. Met me in Morpeth, by appointment. Said he wanted my co-operation. Said if I went along with things, helped in the enquiry into the smokies business, they'd do what they could to make sure I got off lightly with my part in the Ravenstone affair. He said he'd see to it that charges against me were dropped, in return for my help."

"With what authority would this... this mysterious character you met in town be able to offer you a deal?" Spate sneered.

Paddy Fenton hesitated. Eric leaned forward. "I think it's common knowledge now that an enquiry is being held into the development of this illegal industry in the north. Under the chairmanship of Mr Justice Dawson. I'm sure it's been brought to your attention."

Charlie Spate glowered. It was a sore point with him. He had only recently been told about the Dawson enquiry. It annoyed him that others seemed to have found out before he did. "We've heard about it. Are you trying to tell me, Fenton, that you agreed to work for the enquiry? Up to now you been telling us you knew nothing about the business; you even said you didn't know what your barn was to be used for!"

Paddy Fenton wriggled uncomfortably. His tone was sullen. "I said that at the time, because I didn't want to get involved. I had a conversation with Charlton, not just at the market but later, at the Golden Fleece –"

"And was that when you met Steve Crawley?" Jarrad asked quietly.

Anger burned in Fenton's eyes. "I told you, I never met him. But I did know something about the smokies, and I thought it best, after my meeting with the Home Office man in town, this Mr Godfrey, to co-operate. That's what I been doing this last week. I been visiting the hill farms, talking to people, finding out whether they've had approaches from anyone over the use of their premises, or for buying stock to be slaughtered on the fells, that sort of thing –"

"All in a good cause, on behalf of Mr Justice Dawson's enquiry," Charlie Spate scoffed.

"That's the way it was," Fenton replied in an angry voice. "You can check it out with the farmers around the Cheviots. And you ask the enquiry people. Ask Godfrey."

"And you just *happened* to turn up and find the dead body at Auchope."

"I thought the farm was deserted. But I took a look around."

"All in the interests of Justice Dawson's enquiry. Oh, we'll check it out, all right," Spate assured him. "But that changes little. You still had a grudge against Charlton, you're still looking for him, and when you came across Steve Crawley at Auchope, and he wouldn't tell you where Charlton was, you let your anger get the better of you."

"It wasn't like that. The guy was already dead –"

"You let your anger get the better of you," Spate repeated insistently. "You always had a short fuse. I heard that you've been in trouble over your temper before this, Fenton, and that's what happened this time. You had a go at Crawley, he refused to give you information about Charlton's whereabouts, so you beat him, and the red mist came over you... and then it was done. You panicked all right, but not just the day you ran from us on the fell. You panicked when you killed Crawley; you left the farm, but then you thought things over and you went back the next day. It was stupid, wasn't it, just leaving the body there? You went back to dispose of it, when you'd calmed down, thought things through. But it was too late. By the time you got back there, to clear up the mess, it was just before the police arrived in the person of Detective Sergeant Jarrad here. And that's when you took to the fells. That's when you panicked again."

"It wasn't like that!"

"So how the hell do you explain the coincidence of just turning up there when there was a corpse waiting for you, a corpse connected with the man you were looking for, Terry Charlton?" Spate almost bellowed.

"I didn't just turn up there! I got a phone call, didn't I?"

When Paddy Fenton had been returned to the cells Eric Ward had asked to accompany him, so they could have further discussions. Charlie Spate walked down the corridor to the coffee machine, obtained a couple of plastic cups of warm liquid and retreated to his office. Chris Jarrad was waiting there for him, as instructed. Spate handed the sergeant one of the cups, waved him to a seat and took the chair behind his desk. "So Chris, what do you think?"

Chris Jarrad sipped his coffee and clucked his tongue, shook his head in doubt. "We've got forensics still working the place over, but there's been nothing yet of much use. Preliminary reports suggest Crawley was killed about twelve hours before we arrived and found Fenton there. We have the implement used to kill Crawley. Fire iron. No prints, unfortunately. Fenton probably cleaned them off after the killing. Like you said, we might find some DNA, but we know he was there anyway, so the scene is corrupted. So, at the moment..." He stared soberly at his cup. His tone was cagey. "Could be, of course, that Fenton is telling the truth."

"I doubt it," Charlie Spate muttered sourly. "It's all too coincidental. A phone call, that very morning, suggesting he visit Auchope!"

"It does sound fanciful."

"You checked it out?"

Jarrad hesitated, and scratched behind his ear with a doubtful finger. "I been on to Mr Justice Dawson's office. They're all a bit touchy there, don't seem to want to give much out, but I got them to admit that they *had* spoken to Fenton, and that he had agreed to act for them, check with some of his farmer acquaintances on the fells."

"Why the hell couldn't they do that themselves?"

"They said Fenton would be more likely to get answers from close-mouthed countrymen than any of the suits from the Home Office."

"But Auchope?"

Jarrad shook his head. "They reckon they had no knowledge of Auchope, and no phone call was made from any of their personnel. I spoke to this man Godfrey. He admits he recruited Fenton, asked him to go around the farmers. But he denies having made a phone call that morning. So it looks like Fenton is lying about that, at least."

"Or *they* are," Spate muttered sourly. "These bloody cloak and dagger enquiries! How long since we heard officially about the existence of the Dawson enquiry? Forty-eight hours?"

"I'd picked up on it just a few days ago, guv, when I told you about it. And even then I was given the information only because I'm still in charge, running the smokies case against the three reivers. Mind you, there had been rumours... Anyway, when I heard officially, I thought it necessary to let you know..."

"Aye, well... But why would they lie about making a

call to Fenton?" Spate shook his head. "There's something funny going on here. I think we'd be wise not to leave all our nuts in one bag."

"Eggs in one basket, guv."

"What? Yeah, whatever." Charlie Spate took a deep, frustrated breath. He glanced at his watch. "Did we get the others in for questioning?"

"They're along the corridor, guv."

"Then let's go see our friends. Find out what makes them tick."

Mark Vasagar seemed very much at ease. He was dressed in a dark blue lounge suit, elegantly cut: his expensive pale blue shirt was crisp, his shoes highly polished, his dark hair swept back neatly, shining, and his glance was confident, his body language assured. He was a man it would be difficult to ruffle, perhaps impossible to shake, and Charlie guessed that pinning this man down to anything criminal would be almost unachievable.

"You didn't bring a lawyer with you, Mr Vasagar," Charlie noted as he walked into the room.

Sprawled with studied elegance in his chair Vasagar smiled condescendingly. "Why would I need a lawyer, Mr Spate? If I'm invited to a discussion with the police I am only too happy to agree, as a conscientious citizen."

"You remember my name."

"We have met once before; it is enough. At Mr Tenby's, was it not? I make a practice of remembering names. Keeps my wits sharp."

"And in your game, that's necessary."

"What game would that be?" Vasagar asked, injecting

puzzlement into his tone, and spreading wide innocent, slim-fingered hands.

Charlie managed a thin smile. He glanced past Vasagar to the heavy-shouldered man behind him. "The kind of game that requires you to employ an enforcer?"

Vasagar laughed. It was an attractive sound. "Enforcer? Mr Berkley is my associate, but do not be fooled by his rather… shall we say, muscular appearance? He is a valued associate, who has been able to produce introductions for me to a number of useful people in the north east."

"Like Mad Jack Tenby?"

"Mr Tenby has given me good advice, yes," Vasagar admitted easily.

"On how to run the rackets? Whores? Drugs? Smuggling? Or all of these?"

Vasagar raised an interrogative eyebrow. Amused, he said, "Mr Tenby is a businessman. We have discussed mergers, joint operations, but the businesses are all legitimate. I am seeking guidance, that's all. I have not yet decided how much investment to make in the area."

"Other than smokies, you mean?"

"An odd expression. What can it mean?"

"It doesn't mean kipper-smuggling from Craster," Charlie said coldly.

Mark Vasagar's laughter seemed genuine.

But Charlie Spate agreed later with Chris Jarrad that the discussion with Mark Vasagar had been a waste of time. They were both in no doubt that Vasagar had come north to set up business in the Tyneside underworld and that the result could be mayhem; they both agreed that Vasagar would be the kind of man who would severely punish transgressions, for all his charm; they both knew that Tommy Berkley would be ruthless in following orders to the letter, because hitching his wagon to Vasagar's star would mean in due course a position of some power and influence among the criminal elements in the north east. But Vasagar had money and muscle behind him, and he was unlikely to scare easily. Moreover, he would keep his own hands clean: there'd be no obvious links between him and beatings in Benwell, arson in a West End nightclub, or a bringing into line of would-be drug princes along the river.

All they could do was to warn Vasagar that they'd be watching him. But Vasagar was cool: he merely thanked them for their interest, and strolled out of headquarters with an air of insouciance.

"The killing of Steve Crawley up at Auchope, it could still be down to Vasagar… or at least that thug Berkley," Charlie Spate suggested.

"For what reason?" Jarrad queried.

"The oldest. No competition allowed. The whisper is Charlton, Hedren and Crawley were dealing in crack. If Vasagar is taking over the manor, he'd be very keen to make the example, show everyone along the river that it just doesn't pay to step out of line, even in a small way. I think we got a very resolute, committed bastard here, Chris."

"Could be," Jarrad replied thoughtfully. "You're suggesting maybe Charlton is hiding not just from us, but from Vasagar as well. And if that is the case, and if it was Berkley who caught up with Crawley…"

"It could be Berkley who tried to beat Charlton's whereabouts out of Steve Crawley. But there's a flaw there. The phone call."

"Maybe Vasagar got Berkley to make the call, pretending it was an enquiry official, to draw Fenton up to Auchope," Jarrad suggested, frowning.

Charlie shook his head, annoyed. "How would Vasagar know Fenton had been approached by the Dawson enquiry?"

Jarrad shrugged. "There's always leaks." He hesitated, eyeing Spate carefully. "And I don't recall Fenton saying it *was* Godfrey who called him."

Spate nodded thoughtfully. "I've listened again to the taped interview. He says he just *assumed* it was Godfrey, when it was suggested he visited Auchope."

There was a short silence. Chris Jarrad shuffled indecisively. "So meanwhile we keep pressing on Fenton?"

"We keep pressing on Paddy Fenton. Get the lab reports quick as we can. And Chris…"

"Ahuh?"

"Keep the team pushing. I still get the feeling we're not touching the real story yet. Call it just a gut feeling, but I sense there's something just… missing, somewhere. So keep at it."

After Chris Jarrad had left, Charlie Spate mused about it. Something was not quite striking the right note. Something awry. A missing piece of a jigsaw. And his thoughts continued to be further confused by persistent images of DS Elaine Start.

14

A grateful corporate client had, it seemed, deposited several tickets at Victoria Chambers for a ballet performance at the Theatre Royal in Grey Street. Two of the tickets had been passed to Sharon Owen, and she had contacted Eric to enquire whether he would be interested in joining her for the performance. Eric was no great lover of ballet but the prospect of an evening in Sharon's company was an attractive one. He suggested he should pick her up at her flat, but she explained she would already be in town and they could meet for a drink in Grey Street before going to the theatre. Eric booked a table for dinner after the performance, in one of the restaurants near The Side.

They met in a wine bar before strolling up the hill to the theatre. The production and the sets of *The Nutcracker* were unusual, the audience was wildly enthusiastic and Sharon herself seemed excited; when they left the theatre and walked back down Grey Street towards The Side she took his arm and said, "I got the impression you were not exactly enthralled."

"I'm a philistine," he admitted.

"No feeling for the finer things?"

He was conscious of the light pressure on his arm and he smiled. He gained the impression that Sharon was playing with words, and that if he went along with the game it might lead to an entry to a closer relationship. He was tempted, but wary. "I like good food and fine wine," he replied. "And the menu at the restaurant is superb."

He held the door wide for her to enter; the staff fussed

about her, and the menu was indeed a good one. When they had chosen what they wanted to eat, and had taken a few sips of the wine he had ordered, she leaned back and smiled in contentment. "I was afraid one of my colleagues in chambers was going to snaffle these tickets – and ask me along."

"Your colleagues are foolish not to have done so."

She rolled her eyes. "God, and then we'd have talked shop all evening."

"And you're unlikely to do that with me," he smiled at her.

"Well, it's less likely. Though your name did come up at a conference in chambers yesterday morning."

"Oh? In what context?" Eric asked, surprised.

"The farmer you've taken on as a client. Paddy Fenton."

"What about him?"

She hesitated, twirling the stem of her wine glass between her slim fingers. "It was mentioned that he'd been released, after questioning by the police in relation to a killing at a deserted farm on the fells."

"Auchope. Why would it be discussed in your chambers?"

Sharon grimaced. "Side issue, really." She raised her eyes to his. "That enquiry... you know, Mr Justice Dawson."

"Ahuh."

"We've been asked to prepare the case. There's quite a bit of information been coming in from the enquiries they've launched. We'll be expressing an opinion. Not on your client's involvement," she hastened to add. "Rather, we've been asked about the chances of a conviction against certain people, on evidence gathered about the network."

"And?"

She shook her head. "All too tenuous, it seems to me. Anyway, it's all going forward at a pace. Your client... it seems he was recruited by the Dawson team."

Eric nodded. "He was asked to talk to some of the fell farmers. That's how he discovered the body at Auchope."

"But he's been released."

"Lack of evidence, really. He was there, of course, but no DNA, no fingerprints, no clear connection with the dead man. And they can't prove he was actually there at the time of death. Some circumstantial stuff, of course... but they're holding off for now. As we should, really."

Her eyes widened. "How do you mean?"

"Talking shop. It's what you feared if you'd been here with someone from chambers – and now you find yourself doing it with me."

She laughed, held up a hand. "You're right. Hazard of our profession. So what shall we talk about?"

There was no problem finding topics. They spent the next hour in pleasant, wide-ranging conversation, about the performance and the theatre itself, life on Tyneside, Sharon's training and experiences at university, the magically clear air of the fells, the wildness of the coast, the exhilaration of long walks in the Cheviots, the magnificence of the ruined castle at Dunstanburgh and the splendid location of the castle at Durham. It was enjoyable, and easy, and there was nothing that touched upon their relationship. They were like two people on a voyage of personal discovery – learning more about each other but circling tentatively, skirting past, shying away from any suggestion of probing into the nature of their relationship.

But the wine produced an inevitable effect. Eric caught

himself looking at the woman seated opposite him, noting the softness of her skin, the glow in her eyes, the shape of her mouth; her fingers on her wine glass were long and cool, and he could imagine the tips of those fingers on his skin, their caress; the skin of her throat and shoulder was smooth and he felt a tingling at the nape of his neck... Their eyes met, their glances locked. He reached out and took her hand in his.

The mobile phone in his jacket rang.

He laughed, released her hand, fumbled in his pocket for the phone. She raised an eyebrow and he shook his head. "Modern technology has this capacity, to drag you back to reality."

"From what?" she asked teasingly.

"Daydreams." He checked the number that flashed up, and frowned. He hesitated, glanced at her uncertainly. "Would you mind if I took this?"

"Feel free. I need to visit the cloakroom, anyway."

Sharon rose, left the table, and Eric connected the call. "Jackie, what's up? I'm at dinner and –"

"Mr Ward, I think you ought to know. I've tracked down Terry Charlton. And it looks to me like he's getting ready to do a flit."

"Where are you?"

"On the riverside, up near Byker. He's holed up in a deserted factory building; no one's used it for years. I'd go in, but I'm not sure. We've not been the only ones searching for him, and it looks like others who've been on his trail have been sniffing him out as well. And all the signs are that the net is closing on him. Someone else has just gone into the factory, and he wasn't going in making a noise. I think maybe we should get the polis onto it, and fast."

"Have you been in touch with them?"

There was a short pause. "You know I don't like to make too much contact with the polis, Mr Ward. But I thought if I rang you…"

Eric thought furiously. Paddy Fenton had been released; he was still looking for Charlton. If he had got wind of the man's location, he could do something foolish. There was just the possibility that it was Paddy who had gone into the deserted factory. "All right, Jackie, leave it to me. I'll get in touch with DCI Spate. Meanwhile, you hang on there. And I think it'd be a good idea if I joined you. Give me the details of the location."

After Jackie rang off Eric waited for a few minutes, thinking. Then he punched in from the phone memory bank Charlie Spate's number at Ponteland. When he was connected, it was to discover that the DCI was not available. Eric left a message, and stressed the urgency of the situation. He was just ringing off when Sharon Owen returned to the table. She saw the tension in his face.

"Trouble?"

"I'm afraid I'm going to have to leave. I'm sorry."

She smiled her regret. "It's not the first time I've been left in the lurch. Another hazard of spending time with lawyers."

"I'm really sorry about this. About your getting back –"

"Don't worry. I'll get a cab. And the bill… leave it. I'll sit here a while, finish the wine, stare at your empty chair and think evil things about you."

"I can't let you pay for the theatre and dinner –"

"You can. The tickets were free anyway. And this way, you'll owe me. That means you'll have to take me out again, to repay the debt."

Eric laughed, rose, kissed her swiftly at the side of her mouth. Her lips were warm, and soft. "That's a date."

He left the restaurant hurriedly, made his way to the Quayside, where he had left his Celica. Five minutes later he was driving out of the city on the Shields road, heading for the address Jackie Parton had given him.

The factory was surrounded by a high wall but the gate that should have deterred entrants was gaping, its bars rusted and decrepit. Eric was unable to see what the factory had been used for: the sign had long since collapsed among the weeds that were growing thickly along the riverbank. It was on the bank that Jackie Parton met him.

Across the bend of the river the lights from Gateshead glittered and shivered in the dark water. Jackie was standing near the gates, sheltered and half-hidden against the boundary wall. He raised a hand as Eric came forward. Eric had parked the Celica at some distance down the road, as Jackie had advised.

"There's two of them inside the factory," the ex-jockey murmured as Eric came up to him.

"Was one of them Paddy Fenton?"

"I've no idea. I was unable to make out who it was."

"How did you find out Charlton was here?"

"I got the information from Joey Califano and I came sniffing around before I called you. I've had a good look around. There's a river frontage to the factory, and there's a battered old launch tied up there. I haven't actually seen Charlton, but I caught a gleam of light from the third floor up there. Then shortly after I arrived there was movement down here at the riverside. It looks to me as though some gear's been loaded onto the boat, and it seems ready to go. I saw someone working there: it could have been Charlton, but it's pretty dark down along the river frontage. Anyway, he went back inside just before this other guy came along. I had to step back out of the way, keep hidden. So I don't know who it might have been. Did you ring the polis?"

"I couldn't contact Spate, but I left a message. I guess they'll be along soon."

"Like the bloody cavalry, always late," Jackie Parton muttered. "Anyway, I think we should hang on –"

Eric hesitated. "I'm not sure. If it is Paddy who's gone in there... He's got a short fuse, Jackie, and he might do something stupid." He glanced at the illuminated dial of his watch. "Maybe we ought to get into the yard, see if we can find out what's going on."

The ex-jockey grunted uncertainly, but then nodded. He led the way forward, squeezing through the battered, yawning gates, swearing under his breath as the arm of his leather jacket caught on a rusty projection. The yard was deep-shadowed in the faint starlight; the walls of the factory building loomed ahead of them, dark and forbidding. They slipped along the shadowed wall, the bricks cold under Eric's hand. Some fifty yards from the gates they reached an iron door. Jackie tested it. There was a slight screeching of unoiled hinges and Jackie cursed, but the door was ajar. Jackie looked back at Eric, hesitated, then stepped inside.

Within the factory building, it was pitch black. They stood there for a short while, listening, but there was no sound to be heard. Jackie fished a pencil torch from his leather jacket and flicked it on. The wide ground floor of the factory was in a state of shambles, littered with empty cartons, canisters, packing cases and discarded straw, pieces of timber, what seemed to be storage containers, the dry and dusty detritus of months of disuse.

Guided by the torchlight they moved quietly along the floor of the factory. The wavering pencil light picked up stairs at the far end. Jackie paused, held up a warning hand. There was a faint echo to be heard, voices somewhere above their heads, indistinguishable words, argument. "The next floor," Jackie whispered. They headed for the stairs and made their way upwards, carefully, as quietly as possible. The stairs were concrete, dusty, littered. A breeze filtered briefly through a broken windowpane on the bend of the stairs.

On the landing of the next floor there was a similar display of discarded materials. The slim beam of the torchlight picked out some sacks and canisters against the wall. They moved along the wall, the light flickering on the piles of rubbish. "Fertiliser," Jackie murmured. "And those canisters... Red crosses... This is old stuff, chemical waste that must have been left here when the factory closed, or maybe it's stuff that's been dumped illegally. These bloody waste disposal cowboys..."

He stepped across to the grimy windows, flicking off the torch. Eric could vaguely make out his profile as he stood there, in the faint light coming through the filthy glass. Jackie raised a hand, scrubbed against the panes. "What the hell's going on over there?" he whispered in an exasperated tone.

Eric stepped up beside him. Through the grimy window he could make out the dim outline of the far bank of the river. There seemed to be a buzz of activity on the riverbank road; cars were pulled up there in front of the long, low buildings, blue lights flashing. Jackie shook his head in puzzlement, then as headlights lanced through the gates into the yard below them he grabbed Eric's arm. "Hey, look, the bloody cavalry have arrived at last."

A car was sliding up to the factory gates, headlights dimming. Eric frowned. "Just one car?"

Jackie grunted, nodded his head towards the far bank. "Looks like those silly buggers have gone to the wrong factory. Or there's something else going down over there. I think we'd better –"

He was interrupted by a crashing sound from above their heads, men yelling. Something heavy struck the floor, and there was a confused shouting. Feet stamped loudly, and dust floated down to them as Jackie flicked on the pencil torch again. He picked out the stairs, and hesitated, flicked off the torch again. "This is polis business," he muttered uncertainly.

"It could be Paddy Fenton up there," Eric replied in a grim voice.

Jackie looked out of the grimy window again. "Where the hell's the polis?" he groaned.

The sudden gunshot was loud in the enclosed space. It thundered out above their heads, its echoes reverberating crazily throughout the empty building. Jackie Parton swore under his breath, as Eric headed, almost instinctively, back towards the stairs, arm outstretched in the darkness. Jackie switched on the torch again, and Eric began to run forward Jackie close behind, the light dancing crazily on the walls beside them. There was another loud report, a second gunshot. When the echoes died again Eric and Jackie had reached the stairs, but now they hesitated as an eerie silence descended upon the factory premises.

They waited for what seemed like an age. There was no sound from outside the factory gates, but in the far distance Eric thought he caught the sound of police sirens, fading in the night air. Dust rose in his nostrils and it was with difficulty that he suppressed a sneeze. Jackie tapped him on the arm and began to move slowly up the stairs. Eric followed, moving silently. There was no sound from the floor above them.

They reached the top of the stairs to find it opened onto a landing. Eric heard no movement. He glanced back through the windows. There were no longer flashing blue lights on the far bank. Jackie flicked the torch beam about the landing. Unlike the floors below, the area of the factory here had been split up by partition walls into a series of cubicles, probably once used as offices. Slowly the two men walked along the dusty landing, Jackie flashing the torch into each yawning cubicle as they passed. When he reached the fourth of the small offices he stopped abruptly. There was what seemed to be a pile of clothing on the floor, a makeshift bed, a table, cartons and paper packages.

And in the far corner of the office space there was a dark huddled figure.

"Bloody hell!"

Jackie moved swiftly into the office space. He stood over the man on the floor, uncertainly, then dropped to one knee. Eric remained near the door, listening hard: he thought he detected a sound from the far end of the landing. Jackie stood up, wiping a hand on his leather jacket. "He's dead," he said abruptly. "He's taken a bullet in the face."

There was a sudden clattering sound, echoing up from the far corner of the landing. Jackie stepped up to join Eric. "There must be another set of stairs along the landing," he muttered in frustration. "He'll have gone down that way, while we came up. Where the hell are the polis?"

Almost involuntarily, Eric suddenly yelled, "*Paddy*!"

There was no answer.

They stood there uncertainly for what seemed like an age. To blunder about on the third floor when there was a man somewhere there in the darkness, armed with a gun, would be a foolish enterprise. But to do nothing was not an option. "We'd better get the hell out of here," Jackie muttered uneasily. "I don't like the set-up at all. And whoever pulled the trigger on that guy in there, he's gone from this floor now."

He turned, started back the way they came but as they reached the top of the stairs he paused. The light from his pencil torch danced on the bare brick walls of the factory, and in the dimly reflected light Eric saw Jackie's head come up. "You smell something?"

Even as he said it, Eric became aware of the faint odour in the air. He started to descend the stairs, with Jackie hurrying along at his shoulder but from far below them he heard a sudden, violent *crump*. A moment later there was a blast of hot air, that made them both instinctively press back against the wall and then the smell of smoke was sharp in their nostrils.

"We've got to get out of here," Jackie shouted as glass shattered in the windows below them on the ground floor.

They ran, clattering headlong in the darkness to the floor below but Eric became aware of another blast of hot air coming up the stairs, and a dull glow that sent shadows dancing and flickering on the grimy walls. Jackie grabbed his shoulder, spun him around. "The bastard's fired the place!" He swung Eric away from the stairs, and headed across the wide, empty space of the factory. They were on the second floor and Jackie was heading for the other stairs at the far end, down which the man with the gun would have escaped. They ran, stumbling in the darkness, but as they neared the second set of stairs they could see the glow was brightening, there was another *crump*, and a sheet of flame smashed its way through the windows of the ground floor, crashing noisily, billowing into the factory yard.

Jackie pounded down the stairs. As he ran after him Eric glanced out of the window to see the factory yard lit up, glowing eerily, shadows flickering across to the river bank. They were heading down into an inferno. Since the explosions, the blaze seemed to have taken hold in a matter of seconds only, and he could hear Jackie coughing as he ran ahead of him, down the stairs, heading for the ground floor and the doors to the night air.

Smoke billowed up thickly now, and Jackie had dropped his torch but it was no longer needed as Eric heard the dull roar of the fire spreading rapidly, a fireball enveloping the ground floor. They were clattering their way down towards the final bend in stairs, but Jackie was lurching, staggering from side to side, thumping erratically into the wall, coughing and spluttering. Then he suddenly fell, crashing forward against the wall. Eric reached for him, grabbed his jacket, hauled him upright. He slung one arm over his shoulder and half dragged his companion down the last few steps. The doors would be somewhere to his right, but he was unable to see them because of the swirling, billowing black smoke. He was in hardly better condition than the man he supported, coughing himself now, gasping for breath. He lowered his head, crouched low to his knees to reach what air he could, half crawling, dragging Jackie's inert form, over-come by smoke inhalation, across the old concrete floor of the building. His senses were swimming, and he fell. He groped again for Jackie's arm and in a seated position dragged himself and the ex-jockey away from the billow-ing smoke that surged and rolled above them, and the inferno that was raging at the far end of the factory floor, reaching out towards them in long, flickering fingers.

His lungs were heaving; every breath he dragged into his chest was a searing stab of agony, and he could barely see through heavily watering eyes. He had lost all sense of direction; all he could think of was to get away, escape from the heat and the blaze and the black smoke rolling inexorably above his head. The door had to be close by, the entrance to the yard had to be near. With senses swimming he pulled himself forward across the concrete floor, and there was a different light ahead of him, colours swirling and dancing.

And suddenly, materialising out of the semi-darkness and the flickering light there was a man there, hands grabbing at him, pulling him painfully over the concrete floor, out through the doorway and away from the surg-ing, searing heat, until the night air was cool on his burn-ing face and they moved together like some indescribable animal, one man dragging him into the yard, while his own hands were still tightly grasped onto the leather of Jackie Parton's jacket.

They stopped. The fingers on his arm relaxed, the man above him released his grip. Eric lay back, aware of the throaty rasping breath of the man who had pulled him clear, leaning over him. Someone else moved behind his rescuer, he could hear voices but they seemed distant and hazy. Jackie lay beside him, unconscious. The scene was brightly lit, the night sky blurred by acrid smoke, but through watering eyes he could make out the features of the man who had rescued him from the factory inferno.

The cavalry had indeed arrived, just in time.

15

They filed one by one into the Chief Constable's office, Assistant Chief Constable Charteris leading the way with a grim expression on his face. Behind him came DCI Charlie Spate, followed by DS Chris Jarrad. The last to enter the room was Elaine Start; Charlie glanced at her sourly, as though he suspected she was in some way responsible for this sudden summons to the Old Man's office.

They took the seats that had been ranged in front of the Chief Constable's desk. He sat there, drumming his fingers impatiently on the desk top, eyeing them each in turn as though he regarded them as unusual examples of a lower form of life. They sat there in silence, waiting. At last, he cleared his throat, peremptorily.

"Yesterday afternoon I had a conversation with ACC Charteris here and, as a result of the report he has now put on my desk, I thought we'd better meet as soon as possible, in order that I can get everything straight – and you can get *your* stories straight. Before I have to attend the inevitable press conference, and explain what's been going on. But let's start with the cock-ups, shall we? And that means we begin with you, DS Jarrad."

He turned his cold glance upon the detective sergeant. Jarrad's appearance had changed significantly: most of the hair on his head had been singed away, he had no eyebrows left and his right hand was still bandaged. He held the Chief Constable's glance, almost defiantly.

"Cock-up, sir?"

"Just how in the hell did it happen that the cars

despatched to the factory ended up on the Gateshead bank?"

"It wasn't my fault, sir," Jarrad argued in a determined tone. "I didn't take the original call personally. I came into the office and was informed that the solicitor Eric Ward had rung in, to report that Terry Charlton was to be found at a deserted factory on the river bank near Byker. I headed for my car immediately, left a message for DCI Spate, and instructed the front desk to send back up. They must have got it wrong."

"The duty sergeant in question swears that you told him it was the factory site on the Gateshead bank."

"He's wrong, sir," Jarrad replied stubbornly. "Maybe it was a slip of the tongue or something, or he misunderstood me, everything was happening quickly after we got the call but I'm certain – convinced – I gave out the proper location."

"So you dashed off alone."

"Yes, sir. I didn't have much choice. DCI Spate wasn't available, so I left the message, called for back up and headed for the factory."

"Foolish bravado, some might say. It could have cost you your life, DS Jarrad," the Chief Constable suggested, a strange glint in his eye. "It meant you were the first at the scene, as the factory went up in smoke. And that meant you had to deal with events alone. The back up you'd requested was on a wild goose chase, on the other side of the river."

Charlie Spate intervened. He clearly resented the critical note in the Chief Constable's voice. "I don't see how it was his fault, sir. And mistake or not, it was DS Jarrad who was on hand to save the lives of two people."

"Ah, yes, while two others died inside."

"Villains!"

"Even so –"

"He *saved* two people, sir!" Charlie insisted passionately.

"Mmm," the Chief Constable said, nodding. "The solicitor, Ward, and his companion…"

"Parton, sir."

"You've taken statements from them?"

"Of course. They were both suffering from smoke inhalation, Parton also suffered from some burns to his back. But if Chris Jarrad hadn't arrived there when he did, and risked his own life by entering the building to drag them out, there'd have been no statements to take."

"That wasn't quite the way of it," Jarrad interjected in a deprecating tone. "I was still standing there in the doorway, not sure what to do. I didn't know at that stage if there was anyone in there. Then, just as the first of the police cars arrived, it was then I saw Ward, dragging Parton out. I just went in, lent a hand –"

"But neither of them would have made it without DS Jarrad's assistance," Spate insisted. "So whatever cock-ups might or might not have been committed, his bravery should be recognised."

The Chief Constable raised his eyebrows in mock interrogation. "George Medal, I suppose. Is that what you want me to recommend, DCI, for the conclusion of an operation that seemed to be going around in circles and ended up with a blaze that consumed a factory?"

"A *deserted* factory, sir, in which illegal chemical waste had been dumped –"

"Ah, yes, the list of illegal activities in this investigation seem to be endless. What have we had here?" the Chief Constable purred. "Illegal slaughtering at Ravenstone

Farm and a constable almost blinded by a blowtorch. Drug wars along the river. One man dead of an overdose, dumped at a waste disposal site. Another found murdered at Auchope Farm. And yet another in that factory with, it seems, a bullet in the head. And they say it's Liverpool that's like the Wild West these days!" The Chief Constable's lip was curled in obvious dissatisfaction. He had a pending honour to be concerned about. "What exactly did Mr Ward's statement disclose, Spate?"

Sullenly, Charlie Spate glanced at Jarrad. He shrugged. "Ward's statement confirms what DS Jarrad has explained. He says he received information that Terry Charlton – the man we'd been looking for since the Ravenstone incident – was to be found at the factory. But when Ward and his nosy companion got up to the third floor they found Charlton lying there. Dead."

"With a bullet in the head, forensics confirm," the Chief Constable muttered. "Though they had little enough to go on, after what the fire did to the body. And they are sure it's Charlton? We don't want another example of mistaken identity."

Spate nodded reluctantly. "Pretty certain, this time. I've spoken to the pathologist this morning. They've managed to check dental records, from the time Charlton spent in Durham prison."

"So we get *something* right occasionally," the Chief Constable murmured sarcastically. "We keep good dental records."

Charlie Spate opened his mouth to make an angry retort, but thought better of it. The Chief Constable eyed him sourly, and then asked, "And the other body, on the ground floor of the factory? Also badly burned but...?"

Charlie shifted uneasily in his seat. "It looks as though

it was a man called Tommy Berkley. He's no loss to the river. A muscle man with a record of violence as long as his arm."

"Who came to a violent end," the Chief Constable said almost to himself. His glance flickered from Charlie to Jarrad and back again. "Fine. So, I've no doubt you and DS Jarrad will by now have worked out exactly what has been going on to bring about this state of affairs. Perhaps you'd like to explain to us."

Charlie hesitated. He shot a quick glance in Elaine Start's direction. He was puzzled why she and ACC Jim Charteris should have been brought into this conference at all, but at least his account would now show what she had been missing, by refusing to work on his team. It was Jarrad who'd be getting most of the credit out of this operation, for all her sucking up to her Assistant Chief Constable. "It's all been about a turf war along Tyneside," he began.

The Chief Constable's eyes glittered coldly. He leaned back in his chair, listening carefully.

"There's been an influx of new villains into the area. They set up the smokies business, and got Terry Charlton involved in a small way, organising some of the slaughtering. But they have been moving into other areas as well. There's been a lot of heat on the drugs scene in Middlesbrough, and the centre of trade has been moving north. A network has been set up in Newcastle and out along the river. And it's a network that's tight. These new boys, they don't like competition. And that's where Terry Charlton came unstuck."

"And how did that come about?" the Chief Constable asked quietly.

"He wanted to set up his own operation. He got a

source of cocaine of his own, began freebasing the cocaine, started peddling, dealing in crack. But he was still working for the new network, and when they found out about his entrepreneurial activity, along with his two mates Hedren and Crawley, they didn't take kindly to it. The order went out to close them down, and make an example of the three of them. As it happened, Hedren did the job for them in his own case. He overdosed, and died. And that gave Terry Charlton the opportunity to try to cover his tracks."

"He was by now on the run, after the Ravenstone incident with the blowtorch," Chris Jarrad blurted out.

Charlie Spate nodded. "That's right. When Hedren died, in the safe house they were using for their business, Charlton saw his chance. He was on the run from us, and he'd heard that his bosses were also looking for him. Tommy Berkley, as the enforcer, was making enquiries about Charlton's whereabouts. So Charlton decided to buy some time. Hedren was already dead; he couldn't complain about his face being smashed in to make identification difficult. To muddy the waters, Charlton shoved his own credit card in Hedren's pocket, and he and Crawley dumped the cadaver at the waste disposal site, before the two of them went to ground, fast."

"They went together?"

Charlie nodded. "For the time being, it seems. They shacked up at Auchope Farm, which Steve Crawley knew from the old days, when he was brought up in the area. They were safe for a while. But at some point, they split up; Crawley stayed at Auchope, Charlton found a base elsewhere, along the river."

"You said Charlton wanted to buy time," Elaine Start suddenly interrupted.

Startled, Charlie turned to her. "We think they each of them probably still had a cache of cocaine. They were still freebasing the stuff. We found a stack of baking soda at Auchope; Crawley'd been using it as a chemical agent to make the crack. Crawley and Charlton didn't intend staying around on Tyneside, now the word was out for them. But they weren't going to leave all that stuff behind. There was a lot of money tied up in it. They wanted to freebase their cache, sell it on before they left the area for good. Or maybe it was just that they had some other local entrepreneur they could sell to, before they disappeared completely."

She stared at him, made no response. After a short, challenging silence, Charlie went on. "Tommy Berkley and his boss were never all that convinced about Charlton's death, because there were rumours going around, there was still some dealing going on, and so Berkley kept making enquiries. And eventually, he found out where Steve Crawley was hiding."

"About the same time we did," Chris Jarrad croaked, his voice still affected from time to time by smoke inhalation.

"And that would be at Auchope Farm?" Elaine Start queried. Charlie glared at her, wondering why the hell she kept butting in. He looked at ACC Charteris as though for an explanation, but the man's features were impassive.

"That's right. Our guess is," Charlie continued, "Berkley got up there and found Crawley. There was no sign of Charlton, but he gave Crawley a hammering, beat Crawley to death, trying to find out where Charlton had gone. All he learned was that Charlton was now somewhere along the river."

"This is all deduction from facts?" the Chief Constable asked.

"Reasonable conclusions," Charlie averred defiantly. "By now, a lot of people knew Charlton was on the run, there was a deal of talk along the river, and it couldn't be too long before Berkley discovered his whereabouts. It was Ward's informant, Jackie Parton who finally discovered the location, at about the same time as Tommy Berkley did."

"That's how Parton came to be there at the factory," Jarrad added. "And how Eric Ward joined him. He was afraid that Paddy Fenton might have found out and gone there for revenge."

"Fenton. Your earlier suspect for the killing of Crawley. Now cleared of all involvement," the Chief Constable purred.

There was a short, embarrassed silence. Charlie Spate nodded, and replied gruffly, "Everything, it seems, except the renting of the barn at Ravenstone."

The Chief Constable sighed, and shook his head in regret. "So much expensive waste of police resources. And you keep asking for more support… However, go on, DCI."

Charlie resented the criticism but held his temper. "That's just about all there is," he said, shrugging. "Apparently, from his statement, Parton must have seen Berkley enter the factory building, looking for Charlton. Berkley found him, on the third floor. Ward and Parton went in as well, thinking maybe it was Paddy Fenton who was bearding Charlton. They heard gunshots; they found Charlton in one of the offices. Dead."

"And Berkley?"

"He must have heard them coming up the stairs. He went down at the other end of the building. That's when he set fire to the place."

The Chief Constable leaned forward. "With what objective?" he asked, frowning.

Spate glanced at Chris Jarrad. The detective sergeant cleared his sore throat. "We can't be sure. Maybe it was just to cause a diversion, while he got away. Maybe he was hoping to destroy any forensic evidence he might have left behind, after killing Charlton. Or maybe he intended making sure that the two people who had followed him into the building wouldn't be getting out again. And in that, at least, he almost succeeded."

"While he himself was killed," Elaine Start intervened, with a strange note in her voice.

Charlie glared at her again. What the hell had got into her? What did all this have to do with her? She hadn't even been involved in the investigation. He turned back to the Chief Constable. "When Berkley started the fire – for whatever reason, it doesn't matter – he had plenty of material to get it going. Old cartons, litter, rubbish. Ward told us in his statement that the place was a real dump. But what Berkley hadn't realised was that there were some old canisters of chemicals left there. He set the fire close by; he waited to make sure the fire took hold. Maybe he was waiting for the two men upstairs to come down, so he could nail them. He waited too long. One of the canisters suddenly exploded. And then a second one went off and within moments the place was like an inferno. Berkley didn't survive the blast. The forensic people working with the fire service, they found the charred remains of his body. And they found the gun too. We can prove it was the same gun that finally put an end to the dead man running."

"What?" the Chief Constable said in puzzlement.

"Terry Charlton," Spate muttered.

The Chief Constable clearly failed to understand Charlie Spate's reference, but decided to let it go in case he was alone in his ignorance. "So, to sum up the results of your investigation, DCI, we can now assume everything is more or less cleared up. We can expect to have convictions of the three men who undertook the slaughtering at Ravenstone. The man we were looking for in connection with the blowtorch incident is now dead, killed by a member of his own criminal network, so we can forget about him. We've been able to identify the murderer of both Steve Crawley and Terry Charlton – that is, this man Berkley – and he was killed in the factory fire that he himself had started. The man Hedren, dumped on a disposal site, well that was a case of an overdose anyway. And a crack dealing ring – Charlton, Crawley and Hedren – has been closed down."

He waited. Charlie nodded. "That's about it, sir."

"So we can conveniently forget about the cock-up of police cars chasing about on the wrong side of the river, and just think about..." The Chief Constable's glance turned towards Chris Jarrad. "How to avoid getting our fingers burned in future."

He seemed pleased by his own touch of humour, but no one laughed. After a few moments, the Chief Constable switched his gaze to Assistant Chief Constable Charteris. "You have any thoughts about it, Mr Charteris?"

"A very neat package," Charteris asserted, smiling grimly.

The Chief Constable glanced at Elaine Start and raised his eyebrows. "And your view, DS Start?"

"A load of codswallop, sir," DS Start commented in a firm, confident voice.

16

There was a long pregnant silence in the room, during which everyone stared at Elaine Start. The Chief Constable's glance was contemplative; ACC Jim Charteris placed the tips of his fingers together and adopted a wise owl expression. Chris Jarrad seemed turned to stone. Then Charlie Spate exploded. "What the hell is that supposed to mean? Are you taking this conference *seriously*?" He turned to the Chief Constable in fury. "We done a lot of work on this enquiry, sir. That throwaway line was out of order. Chris Jarrad here almost got himself killed. I take exception to a junior officer –"

The Chief Constable held up a warning hand, cutting Charlie off in mid-sentence. His tone was glacial. "One moment, DCI. I think we should listen to DS Start. I've already told you I've had a report from ACC Charteris about these matters. And it seems DS Start has some... concerns, I understand."

Charlie's breathing was harsh as he glared at Elaine, but she ignored him. Her eyes were fixed on Chris Jarrad. They all waited silently. "Shortly after you arrived at the factory," she said, "a police car joined you."

Chris Jarrad shifted in his seat. "That's right," he croaked in reply.

"It wasn't one of the back up cars you'd sent for. They were on the other side of the river. So who had called in this squad car?"

Jarrad shrugged. "They'd picked up a general call on the radio. They were on patrol in Byker. They weren't one of the back up team, as you say. But they responded to the general –"

"So *you* didn't call them."

"No."

"But when this squad car arrived at the yard, that's when you decided to go into the burning factory."

"Yes."

"Only then," she added in a cool tone.

Charlie rounded on her. "What's that supposed to mean? What are you getting at? Are you suggesting this was some kind of grandstanding?"

Her features were impassive; she held his furious glare for several seconds, and then turned to look at the Chief Constable. "There's another question that seems to have been overlooked, sir."

"Go on."

"Where did these three men – Charlton, Crawley and Hedren – get their supply of cocaine. How did all this get *started*?"

"How the hell should we know?" Charlie Spate snarled angrily. "If we knew the answers to questions like that we could close down the whole drug scene in the north east. Damn it, we know the stuff has been flooding into Middlesbrough for the last few years – it's just about the biggest centre in the UK these days. Charlton could have got his supply from any one of a number of people working the North Sea run. You might recall, DS Start," he sneered, "that at the Avignon conference we had a great deal of details given to us about how the stuff was coming in through the ports on the east coast."

Assistant Chief Constable Jim Charteris intervened. His voice was touched with an edge of menace. "I think you're right, DS Spate. We're of the opinion the supply obtained by Charlton did indeed come in through Teesside. But we also think we know who the supplier was."

Warning bells rang in Charlie Spate's mind. There was something going on here that he failed to understand. He glanced at Chris Jarrad but the man's face was expressionless. Charlie waited.

"About a year ago," Charteris went on, "a drugs raid in Middlesbrough went wrong. A boat was boarded. The villains were apprehended, but there was considerable confusion, and packages of cocaine that were expected to be found in their possession seemed at some stage to have disappeared. Most of the cargo was confiscated, but the missing stuff, its street value was reckoned at the time to be worth something between a half million, and a million pounds."

The room was silent, the atmosphere suddenly crackling with tension. "Within days after the raid an investigation was commenced; certain conclusions were reached; further enquiries were made. Like all such investigations, progress was slow. But all the logical processes pointed to the missing packages being the responsibility of one man. The officer who had led the raid. However, before the investigation could be concluded, the officer concerned, Detective Inspector Donaldson, who was on suspension, committed suicide."

Charlie Spate licked dry lips. The warning bells were clanging louder; he didn't like what Charteris was saying.

"It was at that point I was approached by the Home Office," Charteris went on, "to help assist in an internal enquiry, which extended beyond the boundaries of the

Teesside area, and which was to be carried out on a strictly need to know basis. Only the Chief Constable was informed of my secondment to the investigation. I needed support. I recruited DS Elaine Start to assist me in the investigation."

The hairs on the back of Charlie's neck prickled uncomfortably. He recalled the Avignon conference, the way Charteris and Elaine had seemed to have their heads together so much. That would have been when Charteris asked her to join his team. A slow flush crept up his face. He felt unable to look at her, meet her eyes.

"The Teesside people had been able to give us certain leads, and we were pretty confident that the receivers of the cocaine were Charlton, Crawley and Hedren. We discovered that they had a base in Byker; we set up a surveillance team nearby to watch the premises. Hedren was already dead by then of course."

Charlie cleared his throat nervously. "Why... if you knew these three had received the cocaine and were freebasing the stuff, why didn't you just move in and take them when you could?"

Elaine Start's voice was calm as she took up the story. "Because they were already on the run, after the Ravenstone incident."

"So why continue to watch the premises?" Charlie demanded.

"Because it wasn't just Charlton and Crawley we were after. There was someone else. Donaldson's link man. The local contact with Charlton: the supplier. We were watching, hoping he'd show up at some stage at the safe house in Byker."

"And?"

"He never did."

Charlie sat back in his chair, puzzled. He spread his hands wide in a helpless gesture. "So, what are you driving at in all this?"

Charteris had a slight smile on his face; he seemed happy enough to allow Elaine to do the talking. His smugness irritated Charlie.

"What are we driving at?" Elaine continued. "It's the fact that certain assumptions have been made in all this, assumptions that skewed the thinking in your enquiry."

"What are you talking about?" Charlie demanded aggressively.

"You've been assuming that Terry Charlton was running from his employers, and their enforcer, this man Berkley."

"I'm bloody certain he was! And he didn't run fast enough. That's how Berkley caught up with him, and killed him."

Elaine Start nodded. "Oh, I'm sure you're right. Charlton and Crawley were running from Berkley all right. But he wasn't the only person they were running from."

"Who else, for God's sake?" Charlie snapped in irritation.

"From the person who had supplied them with the cocaine in the first place." Elaine's eyes were steady on Charlie's. "You see, it all started that night up at Ravenstone Farm." Her glance shifted to Chris Jarrad. "You recognised Terry Charlton that night at the barn, didn't you? Even though he was wearing a balaclava."

"So, how are you?" Elaine Start asked as she took a seat in Eric Ward's office.

"I've felt better," he replied, smiling slightly. "I still

have a certain problem with my breathing from time to time. Smoke inhalation is not a pleasant experience."

"And your friend?"

"Jackie Parton?" Eric shook his head. "He's always been a tough old bird. His hands will be scarred, and they've had to do some surgery, some skin grafts on his back where his shirt had caught fire, but he's been well enough to call in to see his friend The Colonel – who's out of his coma, and recovering slowly. Jackie'll be up and about and doing whatever it is he does soon enough."

"And exactly what *does* he do?" Elaine asked, smiling.

"That's something you'll have to ask the man himself," Eric replied. "Anyway, I hope you've come in to give me good news about my client, Paddy Fenton."

She nodded. "I have indeed. I can tell you formally that all charges are now being dropped against him as far as the business up at Ravenstone Farm is concerned. It's in recognition of the assistance he's given Mr Justice Dawson's enquiry. It can't be said that the results have been completely positive, but at least he's helped build up a picture of what's been happening among the hill farms, and the development of contacts in this smokies operation."

"And what about Vasagar?"

She glanced at him ruefully. "Mark Vasagar is one of the survivors in this world. We're pretty sure he was behind the setting up of the business, but we have no direct evidence to support this. The fact he employed Tommy Berkley is one thing; it's another to prove that he was involved in what actually happened. No, I think Vasagar is going to remain a thorn in our side on Tyneside for a while yet: he's not going to just disappear into the woodwork. We'll get him one of these days. But not yet."

"Or maybe never, like Mad Jack Tenby."

She shrugged. "Maybe never, like you say."

"So you can't show Mark Vasagar was involved in the hunting down of Charlton?"

She shook her head. "We've got a bit of difficulty there. It's clear that Berkley killed Charlton in that warehouse, but to be honest with you, we've been more concerned with another aspect of the whole investigation. When it concerns one of our own, well, it raises hackles, confuses issues, causes more *angst*... and determines new priorities."

There was a short silence. "I'd heard that Chris Jarrad had been arrested," Eric said in a hesitant voice.

Elaine Start sighed despondently. In her mind's eye she could still see Charlie Spate's face when she had completed her allegations. And she had felt a stab of guilt during her recounting: she was left with the odd feeling that she had in some way betrayed the man she had been working closely with for the last two years. And yet her instructions had left her with no alternative: she had no authority to warn Spate of what she was doing. "That's right," she admitted. "Chris Jarrad's been arrested."

"What will the charges be?"

"Why? You thinking of defending him?" She shook her head. "No, it's all been a bad business. You see, Chris Jarrad's been a good copper. He spent twenty years at Middlesbrough and earned a couple of commendations. But at some stage he seems to have become soured. Maybe it was the lack of promotion; maybe it was he found himself staring at a future that was less than rosy after retirement. That's how he got involved with DI Donaldson."

"Donaldson?" Eric frowned. "I've heard something... Isn't he the Teesside detective inspector who hanged himself?"

"That's right. Donaldson was in charge of a drugs bust that went wrong. A stack of cocaine that should have been obtained at the raid went missing. It was Donaldson who'd come up with the idea and brought Jarrad into the scheme. Between them, they'd lifted the cocaine, stashed it away, and decided it was going to be their nest egg for retirement. That was when Jarrad asked for a move to Tyneside. It meant he could keep a close eye on Terry Charlton, who'd done the deal with Donaldson and himself. But the internal enquiry that was started in Middlesbrough soon enough pointed the finger at Donaldson, and a link with the dealer in Newcastle. Donaldson was suspended. The investigation screws were turned tighter. Donaldson couldn't take the heat, in the end. He hanged himself. But he didn't implicate Jarrad."

"But he was under suspicion, nevertheless?"

She nodded. "It meant they wanted to keep tabs on him, because there was some evidence that the missing cocaine was being traded as crack up here on Tyneside. It meant the internal investigation had to be extended, sur-reptitiously: they didn't want to scare Jarrad off. They needed to tie him in personally with the dealers – and that's when I got recruited into the investigation."

"That night we met at the safe house –"

"It was part of the investigation. We were hoping Jarrad would show up there some time, to prove the link with Charlton."

"So how did the whole thing begin to unravel for him?" Eric asked, puzzled.

"It was that night up at Paddy Fenton's farm. Jarrad was leading the raid. And he recognised Charlton, in spite of the balaclava he wore. If Charlton had just submitted quietly, things might still have been all right, but when he went amok with the blowtorch to avoid arrest, Jarrad knew he had a problem. The hunt for Charlton would be serious, because of the injured constable, and under pressure after he was caught, there was the chance Charlton would crack, would try to buy himself out of the Ravenstone charges by talking about the cocaine he had received from a copper. Jarrad knew he could be in trouble: he'd have to keep Charlton's mouth shut."

"So Jarrad was looking for Charlton for personal reasons?"

"Exactly so. And once the smokies hearings were under way, Jarrad got himself transferred to work directly with Charlie Spate. It meant that Charlton found himself on the run, not just from the police, and Tommy Berkley who was out to make an example of him, but from Chris Jarrad too."

Eric rose, walked across to the door, opened it, stuck his head out and asked Susie if she'd mind making a couple of cups of coffee. She smiled assent; she liked Elaine Start. When Eric returned to his desk he said, "Paddy Fenton will be relieved that he's not getting charged over the death of Crawley at Auchope Farm, anyway."

Elaine nodded. "That was another issue. DCI Spate thought Crawley had been beaten to death by Tommy Berkley, but that was never the case. He hadn't thought through the matter of the telephone call."

"Telephone call? You mean the one Paddy thought came from the Home Office contact, Godfrey?"

"That's right. Berkley and Vasagar knew nothing about Justice Dawson's recruiting of Paddy Fenton. So it couldn't have been Berkley who phoned Fenton, to send him up to Auchope Farm."

"On the other hand, Jarrad did know about the Dawson enquiry."

"And he knew that Fenton had a revenge motive for seeking out Charlton," Elaine added. "Jarrad discovered Crawley's background from the files, learned he'd been brought up on the fells, started searching the deserted hill farms, found him and beat the hell out of him, to try to find out where Charlton was hiding out. He failed. Next morning, he rang Fenton, suggested he might find what he was looking for at Auchope. Then turned up to arrest Fenton, more or less *in flagrante delicto*. With another squad car in close attendance, of course, to make it look good."

Eric nodded, musing thoughtfully. "But Jarrad was still left with a problem. The whereabouts of Terry Charlton."

"Which you helped him out with."

"My phone call to say Charlton was at the factory?"

Elaine nodded, and shifted in her chair. "That's correct. He was told about the call but knew he had to try to get there before anyone else from headquarters. He didn't inform Charlie Spate but did mislead the desk sergeant about the factory location. The back up squad were sent on a wild goose chase to the Gateshead side of the river. That left Jarrad with the chance to head straight for the factory. He arrived there shortly after you'd gone inside, it seems."

Eric grunted thoughtfully. "We were on the first floor. We saw a car pull up outside the gates. And the activity on the Gateshead bank. But then there were the gunshots, and the shouting above…"

"Berkley had finally got face to face with Charlton. I think maybe he wanted to know where Charlton was getting his supplies, there was a fight of sorts, but Berkley then shot him."

"He must have heard me and Jackie coming up the stairs."

Elaine nodded. "So he went down the other stairway. What he didn't realise was that Jarrad would be waiting for him."

Susie Cartwright tapped on the door and came in with two cups of coffee.

"No mugs, this time," Eric said.

"Special guest, so best china," Susie smiled. "There are two calls for you, Mr Ward."

"I'll get on to them in a moment," he replied. After Susie closed the door behind her, he turned back to Elaine. "So it was Chris Jarrad who started the fire?"

She sipped her coffee and nodded. "He was panicked. My guess is he didn't know what might be found up on the third floor with Charlton's body. He'd arrived in time to hear gunshots. Now, he wanted to destroy any possible evidence linking him with Charlton. He struck Berkley down as the man came hurrying down the stairs to the ground floor. As Berkley lay there, Jarrad started the fire, but then was overtaken by events. He didn't know there were canisters of old chemicals there; when the first one exploded, he got singed, and got outside quickly. But he guessed you and Parton might still be inside, and he had to wait…"

"He expected us to die. He never intended rescuing us," Eric said thoughtfully.

"He'd have been well pleased if everything had gone sky high: you, Parton, Berkley and Charlton. But as he was waiting, a local squad car arrived on the scene. He was forced to act because you and Parton could be seen, just inside the doors. So he had to plunge in, act the hero, drag you both out…"

She sipped at her coffee thoughtfully. "But the George Medal is something he won't be getting, that's for sure."

After Elaine had left the office Eric sat staring at his own empty coffee cup, lost in thought. He wondered whether he and Jackie might have made it out of the inferno at the factory, if Jarrad hadn't been forced to come in after them. Jarrad must have been torn; he had to all intents and purposes achieved his objectives, he must have felt he had covered all possibilities. And he could end up the hero…

"Susie," he called. "You said there were two calls for me?"

"That's right." She left her desk, came to the door, stood leaning there against the door jamb. "There was one from Mrs Ward – Miss Morcomb, I mean."

"The other?"

"Sharon Owen." She looked at him with a gleam in her eye. "Which would you like to take first?"

It was a question he felt needed some serious thinking about.

Up in town, walking through the Haymarket, Elaine Start was similarly troubled by personal relationships. She wondered what she should be saying to Charlie Spate when she saw him next. She felt guilty about the way she had been forced to keep him in the dark; even guiltier about the way he had been showed up in front of the Chief Constable. He'd been undertaking a murder enquiry with the assistance of the murderer himself. It was something he'd have considerable trouble living down.

Maybe she could say to him, "Charlie, I'm sorry the way things have turned out. Is there anything I can do to make it up to you?"

Trouble was, she had an idea just what he might suggest.

She looked about her at the bustle of the Haymarket. She smiled to herself. What Charlie might suggest, well, it might be an interesting experience, anyway.

It might even be pleasurable, come to think of it…